LOCAL LILY GOES TO SPAIN

LOCAL LILY GOES
TO SPAIN

STEPHANIE GRAY

Design Grade Design and Adeline Media, London

Copyright © Stephanie Gray

First print July 2018

CONTENTS

This book is dedicated to Robert Gray – 'Da' – who I know would have loved it. He loved and encouraged me in everything I did, and he would have been behind me 100 per cent.
Also to Elizabeth Stevenson – 'Lily' – who would have found it hilarious.

CHAPTER ONE

Shiny red stiletto shoes. A tight dress that showed an ample amount of cleavage and a tiny handful of bottom. Glittery silver jewellery. A real do-me-now outfit. Lily looked down at herself in her boxy chefs' whites and steel-toed shoes, then back at the mannequin in the shop window. It was coming to something when a plastic woman who didn't even have a whole head looked sexier than Lily had felt in months.

"Yes, but can she cook?" Lily muttered as she shut the car door and headed toward Millside, the local restaurant in Cloughmills she'd worked in for four years. It was on Main Street across the road from the pub, a smart building that seated a hundred diners, with a gin lounge upstairs and a takeaway at the side. At this time of day, the village was quiet with few cars driving by. School had wrapped for the year and the rolling hills beyond were patchy white with frost.

Just before she went in she cast a last look at the leaden sky. Snow was forecast for later and if it was heavy it would play havoc with their bookings. The village became virtually impassable under heavy snow.

Inside the kitchen it was warm and bright and there were several chefs already hard at work, prepping for the busy day ahead. Siobhan, the pastry chef, was piping chocolate mousse into parfait glasses. She was a tall, redheaded woman with two sets of gold earrings in her ears and had been at the restaurant almost as long as Lily had.

Darryl, the head chef, looked up from the pass and nodded as she went by, then went straight back to work. A porter was at the sink, scouring pans. Another was dashing back and forth between the cool room and the work benches.

"Did you find the mushrooms yet?" Darryl roared at him.

The porter was new and had the glazed-eye look of someone who'd found themselves neck-deep in trouble without quite knowing how. Once Lily had clocked in for her shift she took pity on him.

"I know where they are," she said, and headed into the cool room, got down on her knees and started searching the lower shelves.

Darryl's impatient shout came again. "And get the cranberry sauce!"

The porter, seemingly overcome with excitement that he was able to do something at last, exclaimed over her head, "I've got it!"

The next thing Lily knew something splattered onto the back of her head. She shrieked in surprise as the cold sauce ran down her neck.

"Oh, chef. I'm so sorry." When she stood up she saw the porter holding an up-ended and empty tub of cranberry sauce with a horrified expression on his face. Lily emerged into the kitchen with sauce dripping down her hat and shoulder and onto her uniform. Siobhan and Darryl took one look at her and burst out laughing.

"Oh, aye, very funny," Lily snapped at them, trying to wipe up the worst of the sauce while simultaneously shooing the apologising porter away.

Between roaring with laughter at Lily, Darryl was roaring at the porter to get the sauce cleaned up. She hurried out back to find a spare hat and chef's jacket and once she'd changed she felt more or less human again, though there was little she could do about the sticky sauce in her hair.

"I'm a mess," she moaned as she came back into the kitchen. "And I'm only just starting my shift." What would Mickey think when he saw her tonight? Then she remembered her boyfriend of seven years would be fast asleep when she'd get in at nearly midnight. He had an assistant bank manger job in Belfast and worked regular hours. This time of year they barely saw each other.

Darryl was grinning at her. "Aye, but you're a Christmas mess."

"That's not comforting." There was too much of the sauce and it had worked its way too deeply into her hair. She'd need a hot shower to get it out and there wasn't time now. Pulling her hat over her head and tucking up her hair she resigned herself to get on with things. It wasn't as if anyone but the kitchen staff were going to see her.

Lunch was a rush of turkey, chicken and beef that kept everyone busy. Darryl was on the pass, coordinating everyone and making sure the meals went out in the right order. Lily didn't have time to think about anything but the plates she was prepping, let alone red stiletto shoes and cranberry sauce.

Usually they'd have a quiet spell to have a quick break between the lunch and dinner services, but at this time of year there was too much prep. The kitchen staff had just enough time to eat a few chicken goujons and leftover chips before they were at it again. As Lily was finishing a piece of soda she imagined what her friend Lorna would say about all these carbs. *"Wheat is basically poison, but whatever Lily, it's your body."* Lorna, stick thin and glamorous, could be so dramatic about food. It was Lily's body, and she wasn't bad-looking, was she? All right, her boobs were a bit on the small side and her bum was a bit on the large side, but that just evened her out, didn't it?

Time was edging toward four pm and they were all elbow deep in sprouts and turkey when there was a bang, and all the lights went out. Siobhan stared up at the ceiling, mouth open, and shot Lily a horrified look in the semi-dark. *Oh, no,* the look said.

Lily returned it. *Very oh no.* If the electricity had gone out they would have to close the restaurant. She ran to the window to look at the building next door. "The neighbour's lights are on. It's not a power cut," she called over her shoulder.

Darryl slammed his knife down with a growl. "Not fucking now." He pulled his apron off and went out back, going, Lily knew, for the ladder to get up into the roof. She glanced at the cookers. Without electricity to run the extractor fans gas had automatically cut off. All the Yorkshire puddings in the oven would be ruined. The cool room and freezer would probably be all right if they got the power back on quickly. Probably. But with not much time until service began they'd have to start calling bookings and cancelling soon.

The chefs watched in silence as Darryl climbed the ladder and disappeared through the loft door. There was silence and then, muffled by the ceiling, a loud, angry, "*Fuck*." Lily sighed and switched the ovens off. What a waste.

Siobhan pulled out her phone. "I'll find the number of an electrician but it will be a miracle if they can get here today."

Lily stopped her, getting out her own phone. "No, don't. I know an electrician, and he'll come right away. He's practically family."

"Oh? Who? What's he like? Is he a looker?" Despite the crisis, Siobhan's eyes lit up.

Lily was scrolling through her contacts, looking for the number. "You're such a horn bag, Siobhan. Now is hardly the time. Anyway, it's Mickey's brother I'm calling, Alex." She'd known both brothers as long as she could remember, but it was Mickey with his lean good looks, wittiness and charm who had stolen her heart. She'd played hard to get in high school, liking how he pursued her, and finally consented to a proper date when she'd gone off to catering college at seventeen. Alex was likable enough, but too quiet for her, though he worked as hard as his brother. Lily hit dial on her phone and listened to it ring, her fingers crossed. As she waited she looked around the kitchen, noticing it had thinned out. All the porters and some of the other chefs had disappeared out the back for a smoke. They knew when Darryl came down that ladder there'd be hell to pay.

Predictably, Darryl emerged a few seconds later fuming, covered in cobwebs and shouting his head off. "Fucking hell! Always at the *worst* possible time! The worst possible time." He glared at the cooling ovens, seething like a bull. "We've got a full house tonight and there's no way—"

Siobhan shouted over him, waving her hands and pointing at Lily. "It's all right, chef. Calm down. Lily's on it and we'll get it sorted."

The call picked up and Alex's friendly voice came over the line. "Lily. How have you been? Haven't seen or heard from you in ages."

"Ah, been better. I'm hoping you can do us a favour." She explained what had happened and how urgent it was that they get the power back on as soon as possible.

"Not a problem. I'll be right there."

Lily breathed a sigh of relief at the quiet assurance in his voice. "I owe you. Big time."

A few minutes later she was standing by the front door,

looking out onto the street and chewing on a piece of nicotine gum. It didn't do much to calm her down and she almost wished she was a smoker still. She noticed her hands, which looked dry and red. *Probably should moisturise more often...ah, after Christmas. I'm too busy for that right now.*

Ten minutes went by and she was starting to wonder what "right there" meant to an electrician, because tradespeople seemed to work to a whole different timetable to everyone else. Then a white van with "Kavanagh Electricians" emblazoned on the side pulled up and she heaved a sigh of relief.

As Alex came through the door dressed in blue utility pants and a fleece jacket with a toolbox in hand she wanted to hug him. He was taller and broader than his brother but they had the same curly dark hair and brown eyes, though Mickey tamed his hair down with wax. "Alex, you're a goddamn lifesaver."

He smiled at her, and then his gaze travelled to her right ear and he frowned. "What's that in your hair?"

She yanked her hat lower. "Nothing. How are you?"

"Busy as hell. It's that time of year. Through here?" Without waiting for her to answer Alex strode purposefully through to the kitchen. Lily looked at her reflection in the glass door, trying to get the cranberries out or at least hide the worst of them, but gave up. Darryl's words came back to her. She was a mess, but at least she was a Christmas mess.

When she came back into the kitchen all the chefs were staring at Alex or calling good-naturedly to him. A stranger among them always stirred things up. Siobhan looked particularly stirred up as she watched Alex ascending the ladder.

The other chefs noticed her interest and called out lewd remarks. "Get a good look, Siobhan? Don't blow a fuse of your own." "Something else need a seeing to, eh?"

Unruffled, Siobhan leaned against a bench, watching appreciatively. "Ooh, what a nice view. Your Mickey doesn't have an arse like that."

Several chefs overheard and burst out laughing. Daryl had disappeared, probably for a smoke, so it seemed they'd all considered it safe enough to come back.

Lily swatted her with a tea towel. "Shh, he'll hear you. And my Mickey has a lovely arse, thank you very much." But she couldn't resist a peek herself as Alex disappeared into the ceiling. It was a nice arse. Firm and shapely, and probably honed by climbing ladders, lifting heavy toolboxes and crawling through roofs rather than by six am jogging, like Mickey's was. But at least assistant bank managers didn't come home covered in cobwebs.

Or cranberries. Oh god, what would Mickey think when he saw her? No, scratch that. She doubted he'd be surprised.

Siobhan and Lily stood side by side in the near-dark, arms crossed as they listened to Alex call down to Darryl about the fuses that had blown and the wires that needed replacing. Lily couldn't concentrate on the details as she was too worried about all the bookings that would be cancelled, all the food that would go to waste and the gradually climbing temperatures of the cool room and fridges.

She was so sunk in thought that it was a surprise when suddenly all the lights came back on. A cheer went up from the kitchen staff and Alex came down the ladder, toolbox in hand. He looked around the kitchen, now brightly lit and the extractor fans humming, and grinned. "That's more like it."

Lily threw her arms around him and hugged him tightly. "Thank you so much. You're a lifesaver."

Siobhan was hovering close, anxious to express her thanks, too. "Stay for some coffee and shortbread, won't you? I'm finished at half-nine if you want a pint at the pub, or you could take a look at my wiring if you like." She gave him a flirtatious smile. Alex looked like he didn't know what to say.

Lily stepped in to rescue him. "For god's sake Siobhan, give it a rest why don't you. Thank you again Alex, I mean it," she said, turning to him.

He smiled at her, half-embarrassed, half something else that Lily wasn't sure about, but when she hugged him he clasped Lily back, one-armed, and then pulled away and said to the pastry chef, "Thanks, but I can't, I've got three more jobs tonight." He glanced out the darkened windows. "If I can get to them in this."

Lily looked too and saw that snow had begun to fall. Thick, heavy snow, the sort that looked as if it was going to settle in. That spelled disaster for the evening's bookings, and after all Alex's hard work, too.

She looked back in time to see the door closing behind

Alex. "Oh, bye Alex!" Then she turned and gave Siobhan an exasperated look for flirting with Alex. "Ah, you're a dirt-bag, Siobhan.

Siobhan grinned, unapologetic. "I try my best."

Fifteen minutes later, the calls started. Cancellation after cancellation. A few tables from very, very local bookings stayed open but two thirds of them were gone.

Darryl seemed to have run out of swear words and glanced around at his chefs. His eyes landed on Lily. "Right. You've done the most doubles lately. Have the night off."

A night off. Despite the circumstances that sounded like bliss. She'd grab a bottle of wine and surprise Mickey, cook something nice for the two of them and maybe put on a dress and some lipstick. *Wash the cranberries out of my hair, too,* she thought.

Lily pulled off her hat, grabbed her bag and coat and headed out. She stopped by the off-license as she went and bought a bottle of chianti, and then drove the two miles out of the village and up a narrow lane to their home. They didn't own much land but they did have a detached two-bedroom house all of their own with a back and front yard. There was room to add to the house, too, if their family grew.

The house looked dark. That was odd. Maybe Mickey had gone out with some mates? In this weather, though, that seemed unwise and out of character. Lily heard a noise like a trapped cat and headed down the hall. The kitchen was empty, and she headed into to the lounge.

She froze in the doorway, and time seemed to stop. She wasn't sure what she was seeing. A person. No, two people, and they were naked on the sofa. One of them was a woman with her back to Lily, and her arse—quite a nice arse, firm and round and tanned golden—was bobbing up and down, and a man's hands were gripping her waist. The hands looked familiar.

Very familiar.

Oh my god.

The woman kept bobbing up and down, making breathless moany noises. The man lay beneath her on the sofa, breathing hard, face flushed.

Oh, my fucking god.

Past the woman's naked shoulder, the man caught Lily's eyes and his hands tightened convulsively on the woman's hips as if trying to stop her movements, but she was too pre-occupied by her bouncing up and down. "Oh, god, Michael!" she cried out.

Oh, god. Mickey.

Mickey continued to stare at Lily, his eyes wide with alarm and confusion, both of them frozen while the woman continued her pneumatic movements.

In a distant part of her brain that wasn't immobilised by shock Lily decided that the woman didn't exist. There was just her and Mickey and she'd arrived home early from work to surprise him, as intended. She held the bottle of wine aloft. It took some effort because she was suddenly feeling very weak.

Even though her arm felt heavy she was gripping the bottle by the neck like it was a lifeline. Brandishing it like a weapon, the thicker end in the air, wobbling slightly.

Mickey tried to sit up but didn't get very far. Finally, the woman seemed to notice her lover had become distracted, ceased her movements and opened her eyes. Seeing that Mickey was staring at something past her shoulder, she turned to look and gasped. They stared between Lily and the bottle with shocked expressions, as if Lily was the intruder. As if this wasn't Lily's home. As if this wasn't Lily's boyfriend of seven years with his dick in a strange woman.

Another part of Lily's brain chuntered into life. *Say something. Someone needs to say something.* She looked at the bottle in her raised fist and suddenly realised how threatening she must look.

Ignore the woman. She's not really there. She can't be there.

Like a gate-crasher confronted by the host of a party and asked to explain themselves, Lily stretched her mouth into an approximation of a smile and gave the bottle a little shake.

"I brought wine."

CHAPTER TWO

Two years into their relationship, when they were both 19, they'd taken their first holiday together. Mickey had paid for most of it because he was earning a decent wage as a bank teller and Lily was still studying catering. They were both still living at home and without rent to cover they'd been able to afford two whole weeks together in the sun. He took her to Greece, to the islands, and Lily thought it was the most romantic thing to ever happen to anyone, sitting in a little taverna by the sea with her boyfriend, eating squid and drinking bad red wine. Quite a lot of bad red wine one night, and they'd woken up with headaches and woolly tongues the next morning. Mickey in particular was grouchy and when they returned to the same taverna for breakfast he'd snapped at a waiter for being too slow with his coffee.

Lily had been stunned. Partly it was the hangover and poor sleep, but it was mostly the shock of seeing Mickey be rude to a waiter. Was this really her kind, affable boyfriend? When he'd joked with the check-in staff for being slow at the airport, was it a joke or was it just rude? When she'd told him she was sorry about his hangover but maybe he should be polite to people serving him he became even snappier. *"I wasn't rude. You're just being sensitive because you work in hospitality."* Ten minutes later when he'd drunk his coffee and she still wasn't speaking to him he'd apologised to her and left a big tip for the waiter. Everything was restored and he was her loving Mickey again. The sense of relief was enormous. She didn't want that to happen ever again.

Except that it did. Not big things, just little things. Being sarcastic to salespeople. Losing it on the phone to call centre workers when they wouldn't process his refund or cancel his contract. Once, even swearing at a homeless person in Belfast when they'd asked him for change. Lily was always able to pull him back in line by pointing out his bad behaviour and he usually apologised to her and admitted he was in the wrong. But it irked her that she had to do that in the first place.

Lily watched in a daze as Mickey draped his shirt around the strange woman's shoulders, covering her nakedness, and then do up his belt with angry flicks of his wrists.

He's done it again, but this time it's worse. Much worse. This wasn't in the same league as being rude to someone in a customer service job. How was she going to fix this situation? This was the man she'd loved since she was 17, who she'd built a life with, taken on a mortgage with, planned to have children with, and she didn't recognise him. She made herself look at the stranger, too, because she really was there. The woman's

22

cheeks were scarlet as she pulled on her underwear and tights, body hunched over with embarrassment. Even Mickey was looking at the ground, though he was scowling rather than blushing. All their flagrant sexual abandon of a few minutes ago was gone. Lily had spoiled their fun.

Mickey looked up and saw her staring at them, bottle of wine still clutched in her hand. His face transformed with anger as he saw Lily staring at the woman's nakedness. "What the fuck? Do you mind?"

Abruptly, Lily turned around, giving them some privacy. A giggle bubbled up and she clapped a hand over her mouth. She wasn't even sure what was funny, but this was all quite ridiculous, wasn't it? Lily giving her boyfriend and his lover privacy while they got dressed after fucking on Lily and Mickey's sofa. That's what it was. That's what was funny.

It occurred to Lily that she might be better off just leaving the room, and when she turned around to ask if she should she found that they were both dressed.

The silence stretched as they all just looked at each other. Actually, the strange woman looked mostly at the carpet, but she stayed stubbornly by Mickey's side, and a little bit behind him.

What's he waiting for? What am I waiting for? What's the protocol in situations like this? Tea? Ambulance? Stretcher?

Then she realized what she was waiting for: Mickey to bundle this stranger out of their house and launch into urgent apologies and pleas for forgiveness.

Any minute now. It'll happen any minute now.

Finally, he spoke. "I was going to tell you. I just didn't want to ruin your Christmas."

Lily frowned. That couldn't be what he'd said. That wasn't right at all.

"It's been going on for about six months," Mickey said, as if she'd asked.

What's been going on?

Oh. The fucking.

Distantly, as reality sunk in, Lily wondered why she wasn't crying, or throwing up. Maybe that would come later. She looked at the woman who was still standing behind Mickey, looking at the ground. If it had been Lily she would have fled from shame by now, but then Lily wouldn't be caught dead sleeping with someone else's boyfriend. Making them feel like an intruder in their own house.

Mickey turned and put his hand on the woman's shoulder. "Will you wait in the hall for me? I won't be long."

Won't be long until what? Why wasn't he assuring Lily instead of this woman? Mickey was protecting *her* nakedness. Mickey was sparing *her* feelings. Mickey had asked *her* to wait for him.

"Of course, Michael. But don't be long."

Michael? What the fuck? It was Mickey. He'd always been Mickey. And what did she mean don't be long? Don't be long until what? As the woman brushed past Lily her eyes flicked up, and she frowned. Lily could see the question in her eyes: *What's that in your hair?*

"It's fucking cranberries, it's Christmas!" Lily blurted, and the woman reeled back in surprise before hurrying out. Lily finally recognised her. It was Kiera McCrary, a girl who'd been two years below Lily and Mickey in school. Lily hadn't seen her in years.

Mickey has. Mickey's been seeing quite a lot of her, apparently.

He seemed to be waiting for her to say something but even though they were alone the words wouldn't come.

"Since when were you Michael?" she asked finally.

"It's my name, Lily. I haven't been Mickey since school." Hands thrust deep into his pockets, he muttered, "You and I aren't a proper couple. We haven't been for some time."

Lily shook her head. Not exactly a negation but a denial of that general sentiment. He was her boyfriend. When had they agreed not to be a proper couple? She'd never thought that.

She took a rallying breath and started her Mickey-you're-being-rude-and-selfish speech. "I don't know what makes you think we're not a proper couple. We own a house together. We're in a committed relationship. This isn't something you throw away on some…" she gestured into the hall, then at the couch. "Cheap fun while I'm hard at work. Can't you see how selfish you're being?"

The words sounded strange and inadequate even to her ears, as if she was scolding him like a toddler who had broken his sister's toy.

"We don't have a life together, not with you working just about every night. I come home to an empty house and you're asleep most mornings when I leave. That's not a relationship."

This wasn't how this conversation was supposed to go. He was meant to rant a bit to get it out of his system, and then calm down and start to apologise to her. But he wasn't ranting. He was icily cold.

Mickey levelled a look at her. "Don't you remember that it was different when we got together?"

"I remember that you were called Mickey. That your friends still call you Mickey. That your brother calls you Mickey. That *I* call you Mickey. And now all of a sudden you're Michael."

"I prefer it. And it's not all of a sudden. I told you ages ago but you've obviously forgotten."

She pushed her hands into her hair, felt the cranberries and swore. For the first time in her relationship she was dangerously close to losing her temper, and she rounded on him. "No. I'm not standing for this. This is not happening. Snap out of it, Mickey. Now."

"Kiera fucking McCrary? Kiera *fucking* McCrary?" Lorna had been spluttering this for the last 10 minutes and showed no sign of letting up. She, Lily and Denise were all in Denise's kitchen the next morning, and the snow was laying heavily outside.

Lily smiled wanly at her friend. "I'm glad you're outraged for me. I don't have the energy just now."

It had taken several hours after Mickey had left with Kiera for the numbness to wear off, leaving her with a sense of vague unreality and confusion. She'd opened the bottle of wine and drank most of it by herself, slept for a bit, and then woken up in a cold, empty house with a dry mouth and craving company. Denise was the most motherly person she knew and Lily found herself on her friends doorstep at nine am and had blurted out as soon as Denise opened the door, "Mickey dumped me."

Lorna had showed up not long after and there was something soothing in witnessing her friends' anger at Mickey. That was what Lily thought she ought to feel, but for some reason she couldn't get angry.

"Oh, I have plenty of energy for it. Kiera *fucking* McCrary. You know she blew Andie Jameson in the school toilets when she was in the eighth grade? In the *boys'* toilets," she added, as if this addition made it extra sordid.

Denise put a mug of tea into Lily's hands and sat down. Denise was a curvy, attractive woman with great brows and an even better talent for listening. She was the first of their circle to marry, and the only one to have children. "You know that's only a rumour. And stop saying the f-word so loudly, the girls are in the next room." She glanced through the doorway to where her two daughters, two and four, were watching cartoons.

"Aye, a rumour, but there's no smoke without fire," Lorna replied, and then hissed in an angry whisper, "Kiera *fucking* McCrary."

Denise cast her eyes to the ceiling and turned to Lily. "Take us through what happened, properly."

Lily took a sip of tea to steady herself. "There's not much more to say. They've been seeing each other for nearly six months. He grabbed a change of clothes and left."

Denise grimaced. "Seeing them doing it to being alone in under 10minutes. That's brutal. You should have called me, I would have come straight round."

The resentment on Mickey and Kiera's faces was what Lily was struggling to understand. They'd been angry with her for discovering them. Had offended them by daring to come home unannounced. Why hadn't she yelled? Thrown things? That would have been a normal reaction, wouldn't it? Or was she too tired from work to even muster a proper emotion?

"Did he give you any reason at all?" Denise asked, offering them a plate of homemade biscuits. Lorna shook her head with a little nose wrinkle. Carbs were a no-no.

Lily took a biscuit and held it tightly, but didn't bite into it. "He said we didn't have a proper relationship because of my work. That I'm working all the time and always home late."

Lorna made an angry, dismissive noise. "Did he acknowledge that his hours don't complement yours, or did he put all the blame on you? Did he ever try to discuss this with you before putting his dick in Kiera *fucking*—"

"*Lorna*," Denise interrupted, gesturing at the children in the next room.

Her voice dropped to a whisper again. "—*fucking* McCrary? Did he even say sorry?"

"No. I don't know. Maybe he's right."

Denise shook her head. "I'm sorry, but that's rubbish. You love your job. He's got a boring bank job that he openly hates and only does because it pays well and he can sit on his arse. Don't apologise for doing what you love."

"It's always the women who have to adapt their lives to fit a man's," Lorna was saying, but Lily stopped listening. It was Mickey's job that paid for their holidays when they had them. For most of the mortgage on their house. Oh god, the house. They would have to sell it or Mickey would have to buy her out. There was no way she'd be able to afford the payments by herself or even want to after what she'd seen. She'd need to find a flat or move in with her parents again.

Another horrible thought struck her. She was going to have to tell her parents. They *loved* Mickey. Her mother especially had been delighted when Lily had announced they were going out.

"Such a handsome young man, but then he was always a good-looking boy. And such good manners, too. He always calls me Mrs Regan when we see him in the street. I'm so thrilled, Lily."

Her father had nodded his approval because Mickey had landed a good job straight out of school, not like Lily who wanted to devote her life to the unpredictable world of catering. "He's a steady lad. Just what my flighty girl needs."

Would they start on about Lily being better off with a more stable profession now that she didn't have the financial security of a boyfriend? They hadn't said one bad thing about her job in years but Lily wasn't sure if that was because they'd come around to catering being a worthwhile job or if it was because Mickey was an excellent provider. They wouldn't outright compare her to her brother, Andrew, who worked in IT, or her sister, Colleen, who was studying at university, but they might start saying things like, "We just worry about you, Lily," which they never said to her siblings. It was true, her hours could be unsociable but it wasn't as if working as a chef was in any way an unreliable profession. People always needed to eat, after all, and the restaurant was doing brilliantly.

Oh god, I can't tell them we've broken up. I'm too tired. I'm too busy.

It seemed she'd zoned out of the conversation as Lorna was now saying, "Cheaters don't say sorry. Cheaters are only sorry about getting caught," and Denise was nodding.

They both looked at Lily, sympathy creasing their brows. "You can stay here for a few days if you like," Denise offered. "I know it's hard now, but it will get better, I promise."

"Or you can stay with me if you want peace and quiet," added Lorna, over the noise of one of Denise's daughters demanding the other to give her doll back.

Her friends' anger she could deal with, but their pity made her feel miserable. If they kept on being kind to her Lily would start to cry and she wouldn't be able to stop. She stood up abruptly. "I've got to go to work."

Denise frowned at her. "It's not your fault he broke up with you, Lily."

Lily resisted the urge to snap back that the mum-mindreading-thing that Denise did wasn't cute. "Oh? Maybe it is. They are stupid hours I work and I'm at the restaurant almost non-stop in December." She scratched her hand over her head, trying to breathe normally, but yanked her hand away with a cry and stared at it. "And I still have *fucking cranberries* in my hair."

From the direction of the living room she heard gasps, and then giggles.

She wasn't just a Christmas mess. She was a mess-mess, someone who couldn't even remember to wash food out of her hair for two days straight. Someone who hadn't even noticed her boyfriend sneaking around with another woman for six whole months.

"Sorry," Lily muttered. "I have to go, they're relying on me at the restaurant. The only reason I can be here now is because the snow means the lunch shift is quiet, but it's starting to melt and they'll need me to go in." She wanted to go in. Everything made sense at work. She'd lose herself in the rhythm of service.

Amid her friends' protests she grabbed her coat and hurried out the kitchen door without saying goodbye. The cold bit into her cheeks as she walked along the street. Work would be a welcome distraction from all this thinking. She'd lose herself in food prep and the energy of the kitchen. No one had time for much talking when they were under pressure so she wouldn't have to answer prying questions.

When she arrived at the restaurant she tied on her apron and looked around the kitchen. Just yesterday she'd been tired but happy, cheerfully knocking out lunches for diners, then watching Alex's backside going up a ladder to fix the blown fuses, averting disaster for the restaurant. If only there was an easy fix for *this*. A tradesperson to call to come and repair a breakup.

She pushed the self-pitying thoughts aside and got out her knives. There was a lot to do. It was Christmas, and she didn't have time to fall apart.

CHAPTER THREE

Lily looked up at the semi-detached house and gripped the handle of her carry bag full of Christmas presents. They were the only thing giving her strength right now. A plan would see her through. A plan, and ostrich-like determination not to think about Mickey. Her smile and these bright packages would fend off awkward questions.

For the whole afternoon?

Her smile faltered for just a moment, and then it was back in place. It was just an afternoon. That was all. She'd been practicing her smile in the mirror at home and it was the best thing she'd made all Christmas season and that was including the perfect beef wellingtons she'd turned out yesterday.

There was a wreath hanging on the front door made from fresh ivy and red and silver decorations. She could hear the Christmas music emanating from within. Usually this would make her happy as she loved this time of year, but everything felt tainted. This was the first day she was seeing her family since *the incident on the sofa,* as she was now referring to it, but she'd try to put Mickey out of her head, for them. She didn't want to ruin their Christmas with her misery.

Her mother Mary opened the door and the aroma of roasting turkey and potatoes poured out around her. Despite everything, Lily's stomach growled. She hadn't been eating properly since the incident. Occasionally she'd have a nibble of chips at the restaurant. Some torn-off buttered soda bread as she hastily headed out the door. Half a leftover croissant. Nothing green and lightly steamed had passed her lips in days.

Mary was a stout, dark-haired woman in her mid-50s who loved to cook. Lily had got that from her, though her mother had been thoroughly bemused that teaching Lily how to make shortcrust pastry at the age of five had somehow turned into a career as a chef. She enveloped her daughter in a sage-scented hug, and then looked expectantly beyond her.

"But where's Mickey?"

Lily found herself stumbling over her carefully rehearsed reply. "Mickey's not—he's sick. Stomach bug. Couldn't come. Didn't want to, um, give it to you all."

Her mother's face fell. "Too sick to come? Oh, poor lad. And at Christmas, too. Is he tucked up at home?"

Lily didn't want to think about exactly where Mickey had himself tucked and nodded quickly. "Yes! All fu—tucked."

She would tell them after Christmas, and after she'd had some sleep and the chance to process everything that had happened to her.

No, after New Year. On New Year's Eve the restaurant

would still be crazy. After New Year, she'd tell her family she and Mickey had broken up. From a distance. A very long distance. Perhaps from Mars.

As she followed her mum into the living room Lily cast her eyes over all the decorations hanging around the windows and stretching across the ceiling. There were dozens of Christmas cards hanging on a string and the tree in the corner was loaded with tinsel and flashing lights. Underneath, and spreading some distance beyond, were all the brightly wrapped presents. Everything looked so beautiful and festive but it didn't do a thing to cheer her up. Maybe on the 1st January she'd feel better, naturally. *New Year, new you,* that was the saying. The Lily that had been dumped would be last year's Lily. Old news. Practically another person.

Her dad Rob was pouring out drinks and paused to give her a kiss. He was a leggy man in a gaudy Christmas jumper and spectacles. Lily would have liked to have gotten some of his height but she took more after her mother in terms of shape. "There you are Lily. Would you like a glass of w—"

"God, yes." She practically grabbed the frosted glass of white wine out of his hand and took a huge gulp. As the cold, crisp liquid slid down her throat she felt slightly better.

This is fine. I'm fine.

"Lily, you look like shit."

An amicable male voice. She opened her eyes and beamed a plainly false smile at her brother, Andrew, who was nestled comfortably in an armchair holding a glass of beer.

Nanna Maureen, sitting next to him, gave him a reproving look. "Now, is that any way to speak to your sister?" Far from being a comfortable, knitting sort of nanna, Maureen was dressed in form-fitting jeans and a silver sequin jumper. Her silver hair was done up in a cloud of curls.

"Least I don't have shit for brains," Lily told Andrew with a grin and kissed Nanna Maureen. She was sure she now had frosty pink lipstick on her cheeks. Andrew's honesty was strangely refreshing. Or maybe it was the wine. But either way he wouldn't pry into why she had badly concealed dark circles under her eyes. He'd just assume it was the restaurant hours. "How's the internet or whatever?"

He laughed. "You still have no bloody idea what I do, do you?"

"Not really," she said cheerfully. It had something to do with computers or networks for a tech start-up in Belfast but beyond that it was a sweet mystery to Lily. It was the same for him. Andrew didn't know the first thing about cooking beyond making a piece of toast and they were both happier the way they were.

Lily put her package of presents down and sat on the sofa next to her sister. Collen was absorbed in a book and had only given her the vaguest hello when Lily had come in. Colleen took after their father and was tall and fair.

"What are you reading?"

Colleen held up the cover for Lily to see, her eyes not leaving the page. "It's about human rights abuses under

President George W. Bush."

Lily, Maureen and Andrew exchanged looks. "How... festive," she said, and Andrew snorted with laughter. Colleen was studying law and took her studies very seriously. At all hours of the day and night. Well, as long as she was happy.

As their mother passed Colleen on her way to the table, she snatched the book out of Colleen's hands.

"Hey!" Colleen protested. "I was reading."

"I'm aware of that, but I need you to help me serve the dinner."

Colleen got up with a grumble and headed to the kitchen. "Why can't Lily do it. She's the chef."

Lily stayed where she was and took another gulp of wine. God, it was fantastic. She admired the table as she drank. Her mother had done a beautiful job with the settings, all the placemats and napkins in red and silver and a centrepiece of more holly and painted robins and red flowers.

"Lily's had quite enough of kitchens these past few weeks, I'm sure." Her mother turned to her with a pitying look. "And it shows."

Lily's hand went automatically to her hair. *Not more cranberries...* But her hair was clean. Her application of concealer must have been worse than she thought.

Colleen huffed from within the kitchen as if she were suffering human rights abuses herself.

Her dad smiled at Lily. "Ah, leave her alone. You look lovely, Lily." And then he ruined it by adding, "It's a busy time of year. Where's Mickey though? He hasn't had to go into the bank, not at Christmas?"

But she was saved from answering by her mother calling from the dining table, "He's sick, poor lamb. Stomach bug. When did it come on, Lily?"

Maureen frowned. "Sick, at Christmas? He's a strong young man, shouldn't be lying about in bed on Christmas day." She gave Lily a shrewd look, and Lily had the terrible idea that Nanna knew there was more to this story than Lily was saying.

"Uh, yesterday. We were hoping he'd be able to throw it off by now." She gave a what-can-you-do shrug. "How's the—"

Andrew frowned. "But I saw you and Mickey last night."

There was a sinking feeling in her belly. It was a small village, and Lily assumed that Mickey was staying with Kiera (fucking) McCrary. Wherever her place was. They weren't flaunting themselves in public already, were they? Oh, bloody hell.

With the lightest voice she could muster and her eyes on her wine, she asked, "Did you?"

Maureen shot her another suspicious look.

"Yes, his car passed mine on Main Street. Gave you both a wave and I could have sworn he saw me but he didn't wave back. Very odd. Did you see me?"

"No, I didn't. Dad, how's the garden going?"

Rob beamed and launched into his planting plans for the spring, and Lily knew she'd been successful in heading off more questions.

For now.

Forty-five minutes and a glass and a half of white wine later it was time to sit down at the table. All Lily wanted to do was eat and listen to her family talk but they all seemed to have questions for her.

"When are you seeing Mickey's family for Christmas?"

"What do you two have planned for New Year?"

"Shall we all have dinner one evening soon? We haven't seen Mickey in so long."

"Has he got that promotion he was hoping for?"

Lily answered in monosyllables. It was good of them to care about her and it was true they hadn't seen her in weeks, but at that moment she wished they didn't care quite so much.

Maureen turned to her. "You're very quiet, Lily. You haven't caught Mickey's stomach bug, have you?"

Something about the way Maureen said stomach bug made Lily look up. She wanted to tell her the truth and she knew Nanna would be firmly on her side when she heard what happened. In fact, Nanna was such a firecracker that Lily wouldn't put it past her to stand up from the dinner table, go straight round to Mickey's house and give him an earful for his terrible behaviour. Lily had to cover a smile with a cough at the thought.

Colleen leaned away from her with a wrinkled nose. "Oh, you haven't caught it, have you?"

Lily rolled her eyes and put another roast potato in her mouth.

"Maybe you'd best stay here tonight?" her dad suggested. "Don't want to risk getting sick when the restaurant's relying on you."

That would give them ample time to ask her hundreds more questions that she didn't want to answer. "No, I want to be there in case Mickey needs anything. I'll sleep on the sofa." Saying his name made her stomach swoop. She shoved another piece of turkey into her mouth.

Her mother beamed at her. "Ah, that's good of you."

Once the roast dinner was scoffed, and a sherry trifle, they all went groaning to the sofas again and Rob poured out brandy for everyone. Lily wanted one but she shook her head. "Not for me, I'm driving." She wanted to know she could make a fast getaway if she needed to.

"Presents!" Andrew roared. "Time for presents!" He got down on his hands and knees in front of the tree and started handing them out. He was always the most excited, and the one who complained the most about what he was given. Two years in a row one of their aunts had given him a wetsuit, and it had become a running joke among them about how he couldn't wait to put them to good use.

Lily delved into her carry bag of Christmas presents she'd brought with her and started handing them out. Soon the living room was filled with the sound of ripping paper and exclamations of "What did you get?" "Oh, I love it!" and "Slow down, you're going too fast!"

Lily had given her mum a new set of ceramic mixing bowls

and her dad a portable speaker for his shed so he could listen to the radio in the garden. They both "ooh'd" and "ahh'd" over them appreciatively, and her dad got straight to reading the instructions. For Andrew there was a hardcover set of the fantasy novels he loved and a white silk blouse for Colleen. For Maureen there was a bottle of her favourite perfume and a spangled t-shirt.

Lily's lap was soon filled with presents from them. Jeans from her mum that were surely too bloody small but Lily wasn't about to try them on with a belly full of Christmas dinner. From her father, a handbag that her mother had definitely chosen. Surprisingly nice earrings from Andrew and a card saying that there was now a toilet in Somalia dedicated to her from Colleen.

"Oh, how nice. Just what I always wanted." She exchanged looks with Andrew.

"Not," Andrew said. He began protesting loudly about the *Cooking for Dummies* book that their mum had given him, saying that he wasn't a dummy and it wasn't his fault recipes were witchcraft written in Ancient Greek, when Lily found more presents being put into her lap.

For Mickey.

As she carefully packed the presents for Mickey away in her carry bag on top of her opened presents, a lump came into her throat at the sight of her mother's handwriting. *Dear Mickey, Merry Christmas, Love Rob and Mary.* That insignificant little label brought her closer to losing it than anything else that afternoon.

Get a grip, Lil. It's just a Christmas present.

She took a deep breath and put the bag aside, trying not to think of the moment she'd have to give these presents back in a few days' time.

I have to get out of here.

A surreptitious glance at her watch told her it was half past three. In about 30 minutes she'd be able to slip away as they all started to descend into unconsciousness in front of the telly. Her dad already had the *Radio Times* out to check what was on.

Mary nudged Rob and said significantly, "Are you forgetting something?"

Everyone in the room snapped to attention, as if they'd been waiting for this. Lily had no idea what was going on.

Rob looked at her blankly. Her mother gave an exasperated sigh, and gestured surreptitiously at Lily.

"Oh! Yes!" He got up and hurried through to his study. He came back holding and an envelope and grinning at Lily. "Now, we've all talked about this as a family and agreed on it, so you're not to get embarrassed or anything like that."

Lily felt her heart skip a beat. What had they all agreed to?

"There's one more present for you, Lily. You and Mickey," her dad went on. "We did want to give it to both of you but, well…' He smiled broadly at her as he held it out. "We just don't want to wait."

For the second time that afternoon her stomach sank, and this time it sank a lot more heavily thanks to all the food.

Something for her and Mickey. What was it going to be? A couples massage? A hot-air balloon flight? Either way she knew she didn't want it, and what if it was something expensive that they couldn't return? Lily would feel just awful.

With reluctant fingers she opened the envelope and slid out plane tickets and a travel itinerary. Alicante, Spain. Oh, no. It was expensive and probably non-returnable. What about Andrew and Colleen, she thought? She looked at them, but they were both smiling at her happily. They were in on this, too.

Mary beamed at her. "We thought you and Mickey could use a break. You've both been working so hard and it's not good for a couple to always be working. What with the mortgage we thought you might not be able to afford a proper holiday, so, well." She trailed off, smiling happily, convinced she'd done a good thing.

"Thanks, you guys. Wow." So, everyone had realised that there was something wrong with her and Mickey's relationship. That they didn't spend enough time together. Everyone but her.

From across the room, Maureen was gazing at her speculatively from her armchair. She knew something wasn't right. Lily hoped she wouldn't say anything.

"The house is on the east coast," her dad exclaimed. "A driver will pick you up from the airport and take you there. It's all arranged. You and Mickey just have to choose the dates."

Andrew was looking up Alicante on his phone and calling

out all the things that she and Mickey had to look forward to. Sun-bathing. Hiking. Sightseeing. Tapas. Red wine. Colleen looked over Andrew's shoulder for a few minutes, appreciating the photos, and then picked up her book again and buried her nose in it.

"It's going to be so romantic," Mary exclaimed.

Lily had no doubt that it was the perfect getaway for a couple in love who were trying to reconnect. Peaceful. Beautiful. Romantic. The only problem was Lily had gone right off romance. Probably forever.

She tried to look grateful as she thanked them again, but all she wanted to do was get home to the peace and quiet.

Mary beamed at Lily. "You can tell Mickey as soon as you get home. He'll be so pleased!"

CHAPTER FOUR

Jenny: *Lillllyyyyy. Please come. Pleeeeeease! You can't be sat at home tonight!*

Denise: *Lily. You need to do something other than work. A night out with us will be good for you.*

Jan: *Gin! Big glasses of gin!! What do you think of these dresses by the way? Should I wear the red one or the black one?*

Lorna: *It's not like NYE comes every year. LOL. Well I think I'm funny.*

Frankie: *Just a few drinks and if you're really not in the mood you can just go home, can't you?*

Lily sighed and closed her messaging app. It was one pm on New Year's Eve, she was prepping for the dinner rush and the girls were blowing up her notifications. The plan was to meet at the local bar tonight to bring in the New Year and maybe try and score a kiss at midnight. If they were single. Which Lily was. But she didn't feel like going, and she certainly didn't feel like kissing anyone.

She turned back to the peppers she was supposed to be chopping. Single. It was a cursed word. Like *failure*. Or *haemorrhoids*.

If Lily went out tonight her singleness would be all over her like chicken pox. She would feel it, itching away under her clothes, making the night feel strange and uncomfortable. She hadn't been single since she was 17. She didn't know how to do it. What if someone—some mad, deluded or blind bloke—hit on her? Ugh, gross.

It didn't matter that than no one knew she was single again except for Denise, Lorna, Frankie, Jan and Jenny. She, Lily, knew, and she was the absolute worst person under the circumstances. She remembered fondly the days when she didn't know anything about any of this. How bloody idyllic those days were. Could she exchange the tickets to Spain for a trip back in time?

They would all know now, all her friends. She'd given the OK for Denise and Lorna to tell the others about her being dumped. Better it came from them so Lily didn't have to witness their shocked, disbelieving faces. They would be sympathetic toward her, and perhaps snarl a few rounds of "Kiera *fucking* McCrary" along with Lorna. It was good of them. They always had her back.

That would be their first impulse. But what would be their second? And how would Denise and Lorna have told the others?

If it was Denise she would have broken the news gently,

as if telling her kids that their beloved pet grasshopper had hopped off to grasshopper heaven (while carefully concealing the fact that the cat had eaten it and then thrown it up on the carpet).

If Lorna had told their friends about Lily's breakup she would have peppered the story with exclamations of what an arse Mickey had turned out to be, and assertions that no man, not *one* of them, was worth giving up chocolate for. While simultaneously refusing chocolate sprinkles on her cappuccino.

She wondered how the others had taken the news. After being appalled, sleek, rich-girl-skinny Frankie had probably announced that Lily was better off without a man. Frankie didn't consider men to be very becoming accessories in her stylish life. She was single, aggressively so, and she liked her alone time. "A potential boyfriend of mine isn't going to be competing with anyone else. He'll be competing with my comfort zones, and my comfort zones have plush pile white carpet; Honey, my terrier; and a vast MAC Cosmetics collection. What could a man possibly bring to that?"

Jan, their most social friend, who had honey-blonde hair and a glittering, dentist-advert smile would think it was a crime that Lily had been dumped just as wedding season was coming around again. She always got a little overexcited during this time of year when invitations for summer weddings started to go out, convinced that all her coupled friends were secretly engaged and about to surprise her with news of their lavish marquee do. Her and her husband, Mitchell, filled Lily's Instagram feed every summer, both dressed to the nines and sipping champagne. Lily didn't understand how they knew so many people but Jan just brushed them off as *connections*, whatever that meant.

Jenny, the youngest of the group with wild curly hair and freckles, would be distraught, but then she was distraught when Lady Mary broke up with someone or other on *Downton Abbey*. "I thought she'd found happiness at last," she'd told them tearfully over wine, as if the show's resident ice queen was her BFF. "He was so handsome, too." Lily could only imagine how she'd take the news that she and Mickey had broken up.

Five different takes on the situation, but who was right? Denise, who had assured Lily that time would heal all wounds? Lorna who swore that no man was worth breaking your heart over? Frankie, who considered men to bring down the quality of life everywhere they were seen? Jan, who would tell Lily to cry more over the loss of this summer's photo opportunities than the breakup itself? Or Jenny, who would want to pour tissues and chocolates into Lily's lap so they could wallow in sappy rom coms together?

As she cleared her chopping board of peppers and turned to the box of aubergines she wondered what they would all be saying about her to each other. In a mixture of Denise and Lorna's knowing voices she heard them telling the others, "Lily *says* that she's all right, but you know her, she has to be the together one. The reliable one. The only middle child in the universe who doesn't mind when good things happen to other people and pass her by. The one who doesn't cause trouble or take the last piece of cake at the birthday party."

As she cubed the aubergine Lily remembered how she'd stood there, idiotically silent, while Mickey and Kiera had got dressed. Even turned around to give them privacy when Mickey had ticked her off for staring. Denise had called her a classic middle-child on several occasions while the others screeched their agreement and she wondered if maybe they were right.

I don't always have to be the together one, she thought, as if Denise and Lorna had really said these things out loud and not in her imagination. *It's not like I go about pretending that I'm fine when I'm not.*

She remembered her false smiles and all the lies she'd told her family, the tickets to Spain that had been hastily stashed at the bottom of her underwear drawer, and winced. *That's different. I just didn't want to ruin Christmas.*

But Christmas was over now, and it was time to face the real world again. It had been six days since she and Mickey had broken up. In those six days she'd had tea with Denise and Lorna, Christmas with her family and worked five back-to-back shifts. The rest of the time she'd been numb, or asleep. She thought about all the text messages on her phone from the girls, urging her to come out tonight. Maybe it was about time she started reintroducing herself into society. Post-New

Year the restaurant would slow down and she'd have to start finding other ways to fill her time. It was probably best to see in the New Year in the way she meant it to continue: with friends, a glass of wine in her hand, and a big fake smile plastered on her face while she pretended everything was fine.

By the time her shift ended several hours later, she'd changed her mind.

Not about going, but about the pretending part. She didn't have to pretend around her friends that she was fine. Most of them had been through devastating break-ups and knew how she'd be feeling. She'd go, have a drink and just try to forget about the whole messy business for a few hours.

And it will be fine, eventually, she told herself as she stuffed her hat into her chef's bag. *Baby steps. It's only been six days.*

When she got back home it was a quarter past 10. She took a shower, pulled on some jeans and a bra and stood in front of her wardrobe hoping inspiration would strike. She wasn't in the mood for plunging necklines and bright colours. Besides, it was bloody freezing out there. She reached for a long-sleeved t-shirt and a fleecy jumper, laced on some boots, dabbed on some mascara and lipstick and was out the door with her coat and into the cab she'd ordered.

She could see even before she entered the bar that it was heaving and the music was pounding. The patrons were three deep at the bar and all the booths and tables were full. It was always like this on New Year's Eve, packed, hot and full of merriment. As she pushed her way through the crowd she spotted the girls, perched on bar stools around a small, high table laden with drinks. They all looked fabulous and were done up in tight black breast-hugging tops or cascades of sequins with heels, making Lily feel short and frumpy in comparison, but they welcomed her with huge hugs and many exclamations over how well she looked, and Lily didn't even mind that they were lying their faces off. It was so good to see them.

Jenny put a huge gin and tonic into her hand with a sympathetic look. "You probably need this."

"Aye, you know it," she replied gratefully, taking a long sip through the straw as she listened to Frankie talk about some handbag lining that wasn't stitched properly. "...and I could tell there was something wrong with it straight away so I took it back. It didn't matter that no one else could see it, *I* would know. I'm not putting up with that sort of shoddiness."

Jan rolled her eyes, but she was smiling. "God, Frankie, you're always complaining." Then she glanced around the bar, one hand on hip, as if there was a photographer nearby ready to take a photo. Jan in her clinging black jersey dress and glittering Swarovski earrings was looking more than usually photo-ready.

Frankie sipped her martini, looking coolly down her thin, straight nose. "I just like things the way I like them, is there anything wrong with that?"

A group of men passed their table and Lorna followed the path of one of them in tight jeans with her eyes. *He had a very nice backside*, Lily thought as she took another swallow of her drink. Not as nice as another backside she'd seen recently, going up a ladder. *I wonder what Alex is doing—*

But she wouldn't think about Alex, because that meant thinking about his brother, and she didn't want to ruin her New Year.

Lorna reached out and spanked one of the men on the arse, and Jenny and Jan squealed in delighted outrage. There was a chorus of male cheers from the next table as they spotted Lorna's antics.

"Looking good, Jimmy!" Lorna called when he turned around, toasting him with her glass. When he saw her he broke into a roguish grin and nodded in greeting, before continuing on with his mates. Lorna turned back to the others with a knowing wink. "I know who I'll be kissing at midnight."

"And then some, I'll bet," Jan added with a saucy wink.

Denise glanced at her phone, to check if there were any messages from her husband about the kids, Lily guessed. "Poor bastard, won't know what hit him," Denise muttered.

"Prey sighted, target acquired," quipped Jenny, bumping hips with Lily, who couldn't help but smile back. She added in a whisper, "You know, I swear I saw him getting off with the girl at the post office three weeks ago. But we won't tell Lorna."

Lorna, oblivious to this last comment, sipped her glass of white wine with a devilish glint in her eyes. "He will soon enough."

It was all so beautifully normal. Frankie was complaining. Lorna was eyeing up the men. Jan was posing as if there were paparazzi taking glamour shots. Denise was distracted by the thought of her kids at home and Jenny was passing on nuggets of gossip. This was exactly what she needed. Maybe it was going to be all right after all. Maybe New Years was about new beginnings, and she'd wake up tomorrow having turned a huge corner. Maybe—

All around the table, the girls suddenly fell silent, staring with shocked faces at something over Lily's shoulder.

"Oh my god," Jenny said, slowly lowering her glass to the table.

Lorna looked outraged. "Who the *fuck* does he think he is?"

Lily's mouth went dry. Her back was to the entrance of the bar and she couldn't see who'd come in.

But she could guess from their faces.

Frankie grabbed her wrist. "Don't look. Stand behind me and they won't see you."

They. Not just Mickey. Lily had to look, and slowly she turned around. She wasn't quite sure what she was seeing, and that alone was enough to set alarm bells ringing in her brain. The last time this had happened she'd been treated to the view of Mickey fucking Kiera *fucking* McCrary. And sure enough, when her eyes started communicating with the rest of her again she saw it was the very same two people.

Clothed this time. She should be thankful for small mercies.

Conversation died around her as the others saw what she

53

was looking at. Lily hadn't noticed it that first night, despite the huge quantities of bare flesh that had been on display, but Kiera was very pretty. In fact, she was a knock-out. Tall and slim, with a golden glow to her skin and a shapely body. Wide-set blue eyes in a heart-shaped face and a plush mouth. A real sense of style, too, as she wore a bodycon dress that might have looked slutty except she'd paired it with a little knitted shrug to balance out the revealing dress.

The girls gathered in a protective huddle around Lily.

"It's OK, love, nothing bad will happen."

"They'll leave in a minute, I know they will."

"That is a very cheap dress. And those shoes."

"Kiera *fucking* McCrary."

"Have another drink, Lily?"

She could barely concentrate on who was talking to her as she watched the *couple* cross to the bar. They were a couple. They were out in public together, not just having furtive sex behind her back. Everyone always said that the other woman never got the man, she just got strung along while he got the best of both worlds: his faithful woman at home and his bit on the side.

They passed by Lily's table and saw six sets of eyes staring at them. Mickey's bewildered gaze scanned the group and landed on Lily. He faltered, just for a second. And then he took a firmer grasp on Kiera's hand and kept walking.

And in that moment, Lily knew. Kiera hadn't been the other woman in their relationship. Lily had been the other woman in theirs.

She turned hastily back to the table and picked up her drink. "Just keep talking," she told the others. "I'm fine. *Please*," she added, when they gave her doubtful looks. Their chatter would distract her from the excruciating knowledge that her ex-boyfriend and his new lover were just feet away from her.

But she couldn't concentrate. Her eyes strayed to the other side of the room and she saw that most of the tables of people were looking at something over her shoulder, and then looking at her, confused expressions on their faces. She couldn't hear what they were saying but she could guess what they were asking each other. *Why's Mickey with Kiera? Did he and Lily break up?* That was the problem with village life. Everyone knew everyone else's business. Everyone in this bar was talking about her. Everyone here *knew*.

"I have to go," she told the girls. She didn't wait for them to reply, she just grabbed her bag and coat and ran out the door, feeling everyone's eyes on her. There were no cabs waiting outside but that wasn't going to stop her. She had boots. She had two feet. And they were going to put as much distance between her and Kiera fucking McCrary as possible. She didn't even feel cold. Humiliation was a terrific insulator.

It was two and a half miles to the home she used to share with Mickey and she arrived 45 minutes later to a dark, empty front room. Midnight had happened at some point during her walk. She hadn't even noticed as the old year slid into the new one.

She'd turned her phone off on the walk home and now she went to the landline and took that off the hook too, and then went around the house checking all the doors were double locked and closing all the curtains, barricading herself in. No one was going to look at her or talk to her here. No one.

How did this happen? How did I not see this coming? And then, more bereft, *It's really over.*

Lily had been good about not crying the last few days but she couldn't stop the storm of tears that overpowered her now. She threw herself down on the sofa and bawled out her anger and shame, because Mickey hadn't loved her. Mickey had only been pretending for a long, long time, and she hadn't even noticed. Mickey had left her for a glamorous blonde who didn't feel self-conscious about being on top or having sofa sex in the afternoon or wearing skin-tight dresses in public.

When she'd finished her sobbing, she went to the fridge and pulled out a bottle of white wine and poured herself a large glass and drank it straight down. Then she poured another and started wandering around the darkened house.

New Year was bullshit. It wasn't about new beginnings. Everything was just the same as it was last year, or possibly worse, because she'd come face-to-face with the evidence that she wasn't good enough, and the evidence had been looking bangable as hell in a size eight dress on the arm of her boyfriend.

She toasted herself in the dark with her wine glass. Happy

fucking New Year.

Lily woke the next morning on the sofa, her eyes gritty and her tongue dry as if she'd spent a night on the tiles. She'd had several glasses of wine on top of that gin and tonic, and it had been a long walk home. All the crying had parched her, too, and as she stumbled through to the kitchen for a glass of water she caught sight of her face in the mirror over the mantelpiece.

Puffy eyes. Washed-out skin. Smeared makeup.

All she wanted to do was crawl back into bed and sleep until she forgot all about Kiera fucking McCrary. She had to be at work in 45 minutes. She took a quick shower, bathed her eyes with cold water and pulled on her work clothes.

Washed up at 25. A failure at 25. This hadn't been part of her five-year plan, an unspoken plan that had, if she was being honest, included a big white wedding, an over-the-top beach honeymoon and getting pregnant about a year later.

Until she'd come along.

Kiera *fucking* McCrary.

The good thing about turning up to work looking like shit on New Year's Day was that no one really batted an eyelid. Chefs liked to rib each other and there was a chorus of "Oi oi!" and "Looks like someone hit the bottle last night!" when she walked into the kitchen.

Lily brushed them off and kept her head down.

It was the first shift she hadn't enjoyed at the restaurant. Even when they were at their busiest, or completely dead, or a table of people ordered well-done steaks *but we're in a hurry* she enjoyed working at the restaurant. It was her happy place.

But not today. Kiera *fucking* McCrary had spoiled that too.

At the end of her shift she pulled Darryl aside for a quiet word. "Chef. Could I possibly have some time off, please?"

He frowned at her, concerned. "Is everything all right?"

One of the good things about catering was that no one let you wallow in self pity. If you brought a problem into the kitchen then it became everyone's problem. Sometimes that made things harder at first but in the end Lily usually found that on bad days she left the kitchen in a better mood than when she had gone in.

Not today, though. Everyone had assumed that she was hungover, not heartbroken, so the others hadn't known not to push her. Now she had to spell everything out to Darryl, and she really didn't want to.

She shook her head. "Not really. I've been doing my best to pretend that everything's fine, but I'm not fine. I'm so far from fucking fine."

He waited, arms folded, for her to continue.

Lily heaved a sigh, balling up a tea towel in her hands. She supposed it was about time she started telling people. "Mickey broke up with me. Smashed up with me, really. Drove a semi-trailer into the relationship and then backed over it again just to be sure." Darryl stared at her, startled, and she gave him a weak smile. "You get the idea. I saw him last night and it was like getting punched in the guts. There's just so much to do with packing up the house and putting it on the market.

Figuring out where I'm going to live, what I can afford..."

"That's shite. He's fucking shite and all. Sorry love."

The next part was the hardest. Lily always hated to ask for time off, because time off was precious, especially in catering. "Thanks, chef. There are a lot of things for me to sort out and I—"

He cut across her, matter of fact. "How much time off do you need? A week? Two?"

Lily felt an enormous sense of relief. He wasn't going to be mad about this. You never could tell with Darryl. Two weeks sounded like bliss but she felt a stab of guilt at abandoning the restaurant for that long. "How about 10 days? I don't want to leave you guys in the lurch."

He smiled and patted her shoulder. "Don't worry about us. Worry about yourself. And if I see Mickey I'll shove a tomato down his fucking throat."

Despite everything, Lily let out a bark of laughter. Mickey hated tomatoes. "Thank you, chef. I appreciate it."

CHAPTER FIVE

The best part about having time off was that she had time to think about everything that had happened and what she had to do.

The worst part was… pretty much the same thing. There was a lot to do, and she wasn't looking forward to any of it. First, her family needed to be told about the breakup, and this needed to happen as soon as possible because Mickey and Kiera were flaunting their relationship in public. It was only a matter of time before news got back to her mum and dad or siblings. In a small village, news travels fast.

A lawyer and the bank needed to be contacted about the mortgage and the house needed to be put on the market. Real estate agents and removalists had to be brought in. Mickey himself needed to be contacted about all this.

Lily gazed around at all the packing that needed doing on her first morning off. *The fun never starts around here*, she thought. Instead, she sat down on the sofa with a plate of toast and a cup of tea and switched the telly on. Then she remembered what had happened on the sofa and switched to the armchair. All those responsibilities could wait.

In the late afternoon she hauled herself into the shower, put on a fresh pair of jeans and a jumper and drove round to her parents' house. Telling her parents seemed like the best place to start. It was easier than talking to lawyers or real estate agents. She didn't need to be professional to talk to her parents, she didn't need to make complicated decisions, and she could cry if she wanted to. The same couldn't be said about the bank manager's office.

Around the kitchen table, clutching mugs of tea, she told them everything that had happened.

Everything.

Mary's upper lip trembled. "Michael was playing around behind your back? Oh, my poor girl. How could he do something like that?"

Lily sat there helplessly, not knowing what to say, because she'd thought the same thing, too: decent, upstanding Mickey would be the last man in the world to cheat on her.

Maureen was there, not saying anything but her lips were pressed tightly together and there was a knowing look in her eye again. "You knew something was up, didn't you, Nanna? On Christmas day."

Maureen nodded. "Yes, I did. I wondered if it was just the stress of your job, but I thought it might have been Mickey."

"You never said."

"Well you don't, do you? You hope you're wrong, and then

when it all falls apart you just help to pick up the pieces. I'm sorry that it happened this way for you, love, but I'm not sorry he's out of your life. Assistant banker," she said dismissively. "What a pussy."

"Mum! Where do you pick up suck dreadful words?" Mary scolded. "Stop copying the kids, you have no idea what you're saying."

"Lily knows what I mean. You need a real man, with morals and strong hands. Someone with a bit of life in him!"

Despite herself, Lily smiled. Nanna sounded like she shared Lorna's taste in men. She probably would have smacked Jimmy on the arse on New Year's Eve if she'd been in the pub, too.

Mum tried to get the conversation back on track. "And we all thought he was such a nice lad."

"I know, Mum. So did I." Bad tempered sometimes, yes. Rude. A little selfish. But this? Or was she kidding herself? Had the signs always been there? Is that how you spotted a potential cheater, by all the little things that you made excuses for but really shouldn't have? Well, she'd know next time to look for these signs.

Internally, she shuddered. *Next time.* There wasn't going to be a next time for a very long time.

Rob recovered first, getting up from the table and shaking his head. "It's a bad thing, my girl. I never thought young Michael would be the sort to run out on a partner of seven years and a mortgage. I never thought. Well, it is what it is and we'll get you through it."

She smiled up at him. "Thank you, Dad."

"You'll be needing your room back, then? I'll shift some boxes out of there today and your mum will put fresh sheets on the bed."

As Lily looked at her dad, tears swam in her eyes. She'd not been tearful through the relating of this news, but his kindness made her want to weep. Asking to move back in had been next on her list and she hadn't been sure how they'd take it. "Are you sure?" she asked, looking between her mum and dad. "I know I'm intruding."

Mary wiped her eyes. "Intruding! You're our daughter and you're in need. Of course you're not intruding. Don't be silly, darling. It's your room and it always will be."

Andrew shouted up the stairs, "Colleen, you're going to have to learn to share a bathroom again."

Lily grinned at her brother, remembering her Christmas present from her sister. "Nah, Andrew, I've got that toilet in Somalia if I'm desperate."

They all laughed, and then there was an outraged screech from upstairs. Lily stood up. "I'll go up and tell her why. And that she needs to shift all that makeup off my side of the sink."

Then she hesitated, remembering there was one more thing she needed to talk to them about. "The trip to Spain—I wanted to tell you on Christmas Day but I didn't want to spoil everything. I'm so sorry you spent all that money and now I can't go. Can the tickets be returned?"

But they wouldn't hear of returning the tickets, insisting that Lily needed the holiday now more than ever and that she was to take herself off in the spring or summer whenever she could get the time off.

"Well, if you're sure?" It did sound tempting, a peaceful holiday on her own in Spain. She could drink wine and read as many books as she could carry.

Mary patted her hand. "Of course we're sure, love. You need something good to look forward to amid all this upheaval."

Gratitude poured through her. She'd been dreading telling her parents any of this but they'd taken it so well she now felt guilty that she'd ever doubted them. She gave them each a hug and then hurried up the stairs to break the news to her sister.

Nanna called up the stairs after her, "When you're feeling better, I'll take you out and we can scope out some *real* men for you. Maybe one for me and all."

Three days later, the home she shared with Mickey was unrecognisable. She'd sorted everything into piles: his and hers. Most of it was his, but the furniture they'd bought together. She supposed they'd sell it. She certainly didn't want that fucking sofa.

It was time to do something she'd been dreading: call Mickey. She took a steeling breath, and then hit call on his name in her phone.

It went to voicemail. She listened to his cheery message and when the line went silent and she knew she should speak, all her words dried up. She imagined Mickey playing the message to Kiera and them laughing at her, even though what she had to say to him wasn't remotely funny. Her face flaming, she hung up, and sent him a text message instead:

I've talked to a real estate agent about putting the house on the market. I assume you want to sell too? Anyway, can you call her?

She sent the message along with the agent's contact details. An hour later there was still no reply, and then her phone started to ring. It was the agent. Mickey had called the agent and put the sale in motion. He was now asking when could he come over to take the photographs?

Lily's throat burned. So, he wasn't even going to talk to her. What a bastard he had become.

Nine days later it was her last night in the house. Most of the furniture and Mickey's things were gone, taken away by a truck, and there were just Lily's clothes, books and kitchen equipment left. Her removalists were coming first thing to put her things into storage and she had a couple of large suitcases to take to her parents'.

She was just sealing a box of cookbooks when there was a tapping sound from the front window. She looked up—and broke into a grin. There, probably standing in the flowerbed, were Lorna, Denise, Jan, Frankie and Jenny.

"You didn't think we'd let you spend your last night on your own, did you?" Jenny called loudly through the glass, and held aloft a bottle of prosecco. The other girls all raised bottles of their own and carry bags filled with what looked like junk food.

Grinning, Lily ran to open the door and they all piled inside in a cloud of perfume and coconut shampoo, kisses and exclamations. It was so good to see them. She hadn't seen them all together since the disaster that was New Year's Eve.

Frankie looked around at all the packing boxes. "Where are your glasses?"

There weren't any glasses or even mugs as Lily had packed them all away, but Denise, ever the practical one, drew a sleeve of plastic cups out of her handbag and passed them around. There wasn't even any furniture to sit on. Taking a cup, Jan wrinkled her nose, as if the prospect of drinking wine from plastic while sitting on the carpet was beneath her, but she accepted a frothy cup of prosecco and sat down cross-legged, arranging her fringed kimono around her.

Then she turned to Lily, a serious expression on her face. "So, Spain? Denise was talking to your mum the other day and Mary said you're planning on going by yourself."

"Which sounds *lovely*," Jenny added, pouring Chardonnay into a cup and passing it to Lily, who immediately swallowed a large mouthful.

"But dull," finished Frankie. "So, we had a better idea."

The friends all looked at each other, as if wondering who was going to speak up. It was Denise. "We're coming with you. I spoke to your mum and dad and they think it's an excellent idea, so if you agree we'll book our flights. Your mum says the house is big enough for all of us."

Lily stared around at all her friends as the idea sank in.

Not Spain by herself with books. Spain with all her favourite people. This sounded a hundred million times better than lying on the beach by herself with a book. She didn't even need to think about it.

"Yes!" she screeched at the top of her voice, and they all let out great whoops of excitement. She held her cup out for a toast. "We're all going to Spain! Woohoo this is going to be brilliant!"

"To Spain!" they replied, all knocking their cups against hers and then catching the drips before they fell on the carpet.

"That part of Spain is just beautiful," enthused Jan, a faraway look in her eyes as if she was already picturing photo opportunities on white sandy beaches.

"Spanish food," added Jenny. "All that tapas and sangria, I can't wait."

"Don't forget the Spanish men," said Lorna, grinning and giving a little shoulder shimmy that made her chest jiggle.

Lily drank her wine and listened happily to all the Spain talk. It had never occurred to her that the girls could come with her but as soon as they'd said it she knew it was a brilliant idea. They were always able to take her mind off things, and in Spain they would have loads of fun, sunbathing and swimming and sightseeing.

As Jenny was pouring the last of the Chardonnay into Lorna's glass, she said, "Guess who I saw last night."

Denise shot her a warning look that seemed to say, *You just can't help yourself, can you, you gossipy thing?* and said quickly over her, "Are you going back to the restaurant tomorrow, Lily?"

Lily could guess who Jenny had seen. Mickey or Kiera. Or both. "It's all right, you can tell me. I'm going to have to get used to seeing them around." *As long as they didn't try to eat at the restaurant*, she thought.

"They were leaving the pub. Holding hands," Jenny added apologetically.

Lily knocked back the rest of the wine in her cup and held it out for a refill. Denise, Jan and Frankie all hurried to oblige her, but Denise got there first, pouring Sauvignon Blanc into her cup. What was this, her third? She wasn't sure, but she knew she needed more.

"He's a total worm," Denise said, emptying the bottle, and Lily took a large mouthful.

"No shame. Kiera *fucking* McCrary," Lorna fumed. "You all know that rumour about Kiera blowing someone in the boys' toilets at school? Jenny heard it too." And she nodded decisively as though this was all the confirmation she needed.

Of course Jenny had heard it. Jenny knew every scrap of gossip in this town. Maybe it was true, and maybe it was not, but Lily found she couldn't care less. It was Mickey who preoccupied her thoughts, and lately he seemed more like a stranger to her than the woman he'd been running around with behind Lily's back.

"You know what?" Lily asked, looking round at them. "I had Mickey all wrong for so long. All the little things that I brushed off as nothing throughout our relationship, I thought they were things that would surface when he was tired or stressed or grumpy that weren't really him. But they were him. The selfishness. The moodiness. That was the real him showing through."

They all nodded in agreement.

"You're better off without him," Frankie said with an angry shake of her head.

"Don't blame yourself," Denise told her comfortingly. "You two were so young when you got together. You can't spot jerks as easily when you're 17."

Lorna nodded in agreement. "And then once you fall in love it's too late. You're blind."

Lily nodded, and looked down into her near-empty cup. She did have to go to the restaurant tomorrow. It was her first day back. Ah, but it was only a lunch shift. She held her cup out doggedly for more wine, and Jenny obliged with a fresh bottle of prosecco.

An hour later the girls all peeled themselves up off the floor and headed home. Denise was dropping them all off in her minivan as she'd only had one glass of wine. Lily was feeling distinctly lightheaded as she waved them off and watched the taillights disappearing up the street.

As she went back inside she saw the near-empty room and remembered what she'd said that evening about Mickey. She'd said it to the girls, but she hadn't said it to him. And suddenly it came to her that he'd gotten off too lightly throughout this whole breakup. He hadn't faced up to what he'd done. He hadn't even said sorry.

Far too lightly.

Anger rose up, bright and electrifying on a wave of prosecco bubbles, and she dug out her phone and hit dial. He didn't answer. She called again. And again. On the third call he picked up, sounding annoyed. "What is it, Lily? It's late. What do you want?"

She took a swallow of wine and said. "What do I *want*? What do I want? Just calling for a chat, Mickey." She said his name meaningfully. She wasn't standing for all this Michael nonsense. "I'm wise to you now, Mickey Kavanagh. Oh, sorry, it's Michael now you go by, isn't it?"

He made a disgusted sound. "Are you drunk?"

She stood up straighter, and said, dignified, "Well, I've had a glass or two of wine. And why not? Because of you I'm on holiday."

"A glass or two, aye."

He didn't sound like he believed her, but she didn't care. This wasn't about her, this was about him, and she was going to give him a piece of her mind now she finally had him on the phone. "You know what, Mickey? I thought you were so wonderful when we first got together. Kind and generous and warm. But you're not, are you? You're a cold, shallow bastard."

"Am I?" he said through gritted teeth.

Lily was getting into her stride and it felt so damn good. "Yeah, you are. And maybe I would have realised sooner if I didn't work so hard, and that part is on me. But even if I work too hard, at least I'm not a *fucking arsehole* like you."

"Lily, you can't call like this whenever you want. You're upsetting Kiera."

The world turned red in front of Lily's fuzzy eyes. Her voice went up about three octaves and she screeched, "I'm what? I'm upsetting Kiera? *I'm* upsetting *Kiera*? Is that what you just said?" She jabbed a thumb at her chest. "*I'm* the one who was your girlfriend, Mickey. *I'm* the one who was treated to the sight of you two fucking on our sofa. *I'm* the one who deserves to get upset."

"Lily—"

But she wasn't going to let him steamroller over her tonight. She wasn't going to hold back any longer. It was all over and she was going to show him exactly how much he'd hurt her by this betrayal. It felt so good to finally let herself off the leash and let him have it. "*I'm* the one who was cheated on and now has to watch you two parade around the village without any fucking shame. So, answer me this, *Mickey:* what's so special about this Kiera, apart from her tits and arse and loose morals? What's so special about her?" She had started this rant sounding defiant but now there was a distinct wobble in her voice. "What's she got that I haven't?"

There was a cold silence. Then he said in a seething voice, "Take a look at yourself, Lily. A long, hard, look at yourself. Then you might find the answer."

There was a beep, and the line went dead.

Lily stared at the phone in her hand, uncomprehending. What the hell was that supposed to mean?

As she poured herself another cup of wine from the leftover bottles, still fuming, she caught sight of herself in the mirror on the wall. Her hair was a stringy mess in an askew ponytail. Her jeans didn't fit that well over her thick thighs and hips. Her hands were dry and chapped. No makeup. Split ends. Washed-out skin.

Was this what he'd meant? That she was an overweight, frumpy mess, and that was why he'd dumped her? How *shallow* of him. How pathetic, him with his fancy bank job and sudden need to be called Michael, not Mickey. Nanna was right, he wasn't a proper man. Real men didn't put their dick in something else because you had a few split ends.

She put the wine down and walked over to the mirror, looking at herself properly as she hadn't done in a long time. All right, if she was honest with herself she was overweight and frumpy. Suddenly she couldn't help comparing herself to the beautiful, well dressed and slim Kiera as she'd seen her on New Year's Eve. Of course Mickey was wrong for cheating on her, but in reality, all right, Kiera was attractive. More attractive than she was at this moment.

Lily tugged on her jumper, turning this way and that as she looked at her reflection. None of the girls had said anything to her because they were too kind, but she had let herself go badly these last few years. The things she ate, the things she wore.

Suddenly, she was tired of it. She deserved to look like a

knockout, too, didn't she? And what's more she was going to. It just required a bit of work. It wasn't magic, it was just grooming and good habits after all. She pictured herself stepping off the plane in Spain in a few months' time, tanned and slim and made up. Yes, that was what was going to happen. When she got to Spain, she'd look like a fucking knockout.

Lily took a swig of wine and looked herself dead in the eye in the mirror and nodded. She'd show Mickey. She'd show everyone.

CHAPTER SIX

"Lorna, how do you get in shape really fast?" Lily asked as soon as her friend picked up the phone. It was the next morning and Lily was driving to work feeling slightly ropey but determined. As soon as her shift was over she was beginning Project New Lily. This arse had to go.

Lorna's voice was brisk. "How fast?"

"Two days or less."

There was a clacking sound over the phone as if Lorna was typing. She was a receptionist at a dentist in the next village. "Lily, you listen to me. A fitness regime requires commitment and a serious attitude. Are you going to be serious about this?"

"Yes, yes, I'm going to be serious. I want the whole regime. I'm in this for the long haul. When we get to that poolside in Spain I want to be able to bounce coins off my arse."

"We can do that. If you'll just sign here and here."

"What?"

"I was talking to a patient. All right Lily, I'll give you the eating plan that worked for me and you can cook for both of us. Meet me at the local gym tonight. I'll introduce you to my PT."

"Your what?"

Lorna sighed. *"My personal trainer,* Lily. It's not like I'm speaking a foreign language."

She may as well be. Lily hadn't set foot in a gym for years. She knew how to ride a stationary bike and do a fast walk on the treadmill but all the machines and devices were baffling to her.

"Is this in preparation for Spain?" Lorna asked, and Lily made a vague sound. Spain was the deadline but it wasn't the catalyst. "You can start part of your diet plan right now: nothing from that fryer goes in your mouth today, all right?"

And with that Lorna hung up. Lily laughed and pulled her hands-free set from her ear. She could just imagine what the other chefs would say if they saw her making a salad and eating it for her own lunch. *Oh, Your Majesty, a salad! Normal food not good enough for you anymore?*

There was a chorus of greetings from the chefs as she entered the kitchen but everyone fell silent surprisingly quickly. She worked close to Siobhan, and when an hour had gone past and no one had asked any personal questions she leaned over to the other woman and whispered, "No one's mentioning Mickey?"

Siobhan nodded. "Aye. That's because Darryl told us this morning he'd up-end the first person who said his name into a tub of cranberry sauce."

Lily grinned, remembering the cranberry sauce that had coated her head just before Christmas. "I guess that means me. I just mentioned him."

Siobhan thought for a second, her face blank, and then she started to laugh. "Oh, aye, it's you! Don't worry, I won't tell on you." She paused, thinking. "How are you though, honestly?"

Lily wrinkled her nose and shrugged. "You know. Shit." Then she added brightly, "But I've got a plan to move on." She told Siobhan about the trip to Spain with the girls and how a brand-new Lily would be getting on that plane. "If I could just get my energy up for a proper workout, you know? It's tiring being a chef."

Siobhan nodded approvingly. "I've got just the thing for you. It's in the car. I'll fetch it for you as soon as I get a minute."

When the lunch shift was winding down Siobhan disappeared, then came back a few minutes later with a black plastic jar in her hands.

"It's called pre-workout. You take some in water before you hit the gym and it just makes everything so much easier. You've got energy, you're focused, you're strong and I swear, the pounds just melt off you. I hit my goal weight a while back and I don't need it anymore."

Lily took it and looked at the label. *Unleash your peak performance*, read the label. Pounds just melt off? She liked the sound of that. "This is *exactly* what I need, Siobhan," she enthused. "Diet and exercise combined with modern science.

I knew it couldn't still be all carrot sticks and starvation." She pictured herself at the gym later tonight, lifting barbells like they were nothing and impressing Lorna and her fancy PT. With this it was going to be so much easier.

Before she left work, Lily got a big cup of water and unscrewed the tub of pre-workout. Inside was a lot of beige powder and a scoop. The instructions had said something about putting one scoop in 250 millilitres of water, but this was a big plastic cup that held 700 or 800millilitres. One scoop was going to get lost. She added a few scoops and gave it a stir. It didn't look like much, so she added a couple more. There was no problem about overdoing it. She wasn't some part-timer. Lily was about to become a serious gym bunny and that meant she needed some serious pre-workout.

She put the cup to her lips and started to drink. It tasted like overly sweet synthetic pineapple with some chemical overtones. In short, pretty gross. But that could only mean it was doing her some good. It took a few goes, gasping between mouthfuls and pulling faces at the taste, but she got it all down her. Lily nodded decisively and screwed the cap back on the tub, feeling better than she had in weeks. New Year, new Lily. Things were getting off to a grand start.

The gym was at the other end of the village and once she'd dropped by her parents' house to change into her gym clothes Lily drove her car down and parked. Nothing was happening yet as far as unleashing her peak performance went, but maybe she needed to actually have the weights in her hands for the mixture to be activated.

Lorna was waiting for her out front in form-fitting Lycra and her blonde hair in a high ponytail, the epitome of the honed and toned gym-goer. She held a fancy water bottle with something long and purple on the inside.

Lily examined it more closely. "Is that a rock in your water?"

"It's an amethyst. Amethyst is detoxifying."

"How much did that set you back?"

Lorna looked prim, like she didn't want to answer. "£70. But it's worth every penny in the long run." She gave Lily, who was struggling not to laugh, a hard look. "If you're not going to take this seriously—"

"No, no, I am." It was tempting to tell Lorna right then and there about the pre-workout, to show her friend just how seriously she was taking this, but she'd keep it as a surprise. Once Lorna and her personal trainer were telling her how impressed they were with her core, whatever that was, she'd modestly slip it into the conversation. They'd look at each other knowingly and nod, and say that Lily clearly had the instincts of an athlete.

There was a spring in her step as she went through the glass doors. Was the pre-workout finally working? She couldn't tell, and maybe she was just happy to be here. This was about to become her second home, after all, and the start of her new journey and a new Lily.

It was cool and bright inside the gym, and everything was surgically clean. Lorna got Lily a free visitor's pass from reception as it was her first time, and then they pushed through another set of glass doors into the gym itself where they were greeted by a six-foot-two wall of muscle.

"Jonathon!" Lorna trilled, smiling up at this pillar of human flesh. "A new client for you. Meet Lily. I thought you could take her through my workout with me and then we'd get her signed up."

Jonathon greeted Lily with a smile and a handshake that engulfed her own hand. "Have you been to the gym before?"

"Oh, now and then, you know," Lily said airily, bouncing on her toes. "But I'm ready for a commitment and I'm ready to shift this arse and tighten these thighs."

"Excellent!" He clapped his hands together. "Let's get you ladies started. Onto the bikes for a five-minute warm-up." Jonathon showed Lily how to adjust the seat to her height and the buttons to press to change the resistance. "Just a nice easy five out of 10 to begin with."

She looked into the mirror in front of her and Lorna and grinned at her friend's reflection. This was great. She was feeling so healthy already. By the end of the five minutes her heart was beating a little faster and the heat was rising, but that was to be expected when you exercised.

Jonathon had them do sets of standing lunges next, explaining to Lily that it was best for fitness and fat burning to work on your muscle groups first and then blast your cardio at the end. "Don't feel you need to keep up with Lorna," he said, beaming at her. "She's a lot more experienced, but we'll get you there too."

But Lily found she had no problem keeping up with Lorna. It was the pre-workout beginning to take effect, but she said airily to Jonathon, "I'm fine! I'm a chef so I'm on my feet all day." She patted her thighs. "Strong legs. I got this."

Next, he had them do sets of squats, bicep curls, lateral pull-downs and burpees. Lily had broken a sweat and she was starting to feel the burn right through her body.

Lorna gave her a worried look. "Take it easy, Lil. You won't be able to get out of bed tomorrow you'll be so stiff."

"I'm fine!" she said, doing another jumping jack and plank combo. Burpee. That was a funny name for this exercise. Burpee. Burpee. "I'm absolutely fine!"

In fact, she was starting to feel a bit lightheaded. Like her heart might be racing a bit too much, but that was probably just how people felt when they worked out. She'd done a bit of PE at school but that was pretty much the last time she'd broken a sweat in the gym.

I'm going to look so fabulous in Spain, she told her reflection with a broad grin. *Toned, slim, and smoking hot. I'll have to get some of that Lycra gear that Lorna has on. It's looks the part. Soon I'll go for morning runs and I won't even get winded. I'll run up 10 flights of stairs.* Lily felt like she could run up 20 right now. This pre-workout was amazing! *I must thank Siobhan tomorrow,* she thought.

Jonathon had Lorna work on the kettle bells next, telling Lily she could skip this one and go straight to cardio if she liked. But Lily insisted on doing this exercise, too.

"I'm not going to get a tight arse skipping exercises, am I?" she laughed.

Jonathon showed her how to hold the heavy kettle bell with two hands, squat, and then lift the bell straight out in front of her as she straightened her legs.

"Squat, fling. Got it!" she said, beginning to do reps. Wow it was bright in here. She saw her reflection in the glass doors in front of her. *Squat, fling.* She was like a machine. A robot without an off switch. Distantly she wondered if she might have taken too much pre-workout. She was starting to feel very strange.

Jonathon eyed her carefully as she squatted and flung, and said, "I really think you should stop, Lily. Save something for another day."

"I'm fine! I don't want to stop!" But Lily had the terrible feeling that she couldn't stop if she tried. *Squat, fling. Squat, fling.* On and on, over and over. *Squat, fling.* Lorna had finished her reps but Lily was still going. *Squat, fling.*

A voice came down a long tunnel. "Lily, you can stop now. Lily?"

The world was getting very dark. *Squat, fling.*

She couldn't stop. She was a machine. A robot set to go faster and faster. Her body was a jet-fuelled dynamo ready to propel her to the moon.

She should probably stop. *Squat, fling.*

She couldn't stop! *Squat, fling.*

HELP! *Squat, FLING.*

"Lily?"

As Lily opened her eyes she saw that Lorna was bending over her, her face creased with worry. "She's awake. Oh my god, Lily. We told you to stop. Why didn't you stop? You nearly bloody killed yourself."

Jonathon's face joined Lorna's, similarly creased. "Don't try to get up. The ambulance is on its way."

Ambulance? She could feel her heart pounding at 500 miles an hour and she was flat on her back, looking up at the gym ceiling. What the hell happened? What was she doing on the floor?

The personal trainer glanced at Lorna. "Is she on anything?"

Lorna looked offended. "Of course she's not *on anything.* Don't be silly."

"Pre-workout," Lily mumbled. This wasn't what she'd imagined happening when she confessed to using pre-workout. Jonathon and Lorna were meant to exchange looks, but impressed looks. Not horrified looks as they were now.

"Jesus. How much did you take?" Lorna asked.

"Five...maybe six scoops."

"Six? Are you insane? Oh my *god*, Lily. No wonder you passed out."

Lorna drifted in and out of focus and Lily closed her eyes. There was the sound of distant sirens, and then the next thing she knew there were paramedics crouching over her, taking

LOCAL LILY GOES TO SPAIN

her blood pressure and measuring her pulse. Then she was being lifted onto a stretcher. She opened her eyes to say sorry to Jonathon for causing a scene at his gym, but noticed that the paramedics were walking strangely as they carried her, as if they were walking over something very carefully. There was a crunching sound, too.

She looked down and saw broken glass. Both doors into the gym had been shattered and she saw a kettle bell lying amid all the shards of safety glass. How did...?

Squat, FLING.

Oh, no, what have I done? Her head was sore. Must be from when she fell.

Lorna rode with Lily in the back of the ambulance to hospital, stroking Lily's hair back from her sweaty forehead, her brow still creased with worry.

"She'll be all right," a handsome, smiling paramedic assured Lorna. When Lorna saw him she did a double-take, straightening a little and dimpling at him.

Lily rolled her eyes. "For fuck's suck, Lorna I'm in crisis here."

"Yes! Sorry!" Lorna said, turning back to her. But she continued to shoot flirty looks at the paramedic. She just couldn't help herself.

Lily's heartrate felt like it was finally starting to go back to normal, but that just meant that reality was rushing back. That last huge fling of the kettle bell as she'd passed out—the bell must have slipped out of her hands and gone flying straight through the glass doors. No wonder Lorna and Jonathon had looked so concerned when she'd come around. What a sight it must have been.

"Oh, god, I smashed up the place. I don't think I want to go back to that gym, Lorna," she croaked.

Lorna tore her eyes away from the paramedic and looked down at her. She shook her head, rueful. "After what you did, my love, I don't think they'll let you come back."

"What an embarrassment. Everyone's going to be laughing about this forever, aren't they?"

Lorna shook her head. "Oh, no, love. What could people possibly find funny about this?"

CHAPTER SEVEN

"It's *not* funny." Lily looked around Denise's kitchen table at her friends, scowling over her mug of tea at them. Jan and Frankie were shaking with laughter. Denise seemed to be caught between sympathy and bursting out laughing herself.

"Oh, but it is, Lily," Jan hiccupped, wiping away a tear with manicured fingers. Little silver jewels edged her cuticles, something that Lily found pretty but stupidly impractical. If she got that sort of manicure she could imagine the jewels all falling off into someone's dinner as she cooked.

"Your first time at the gym and you smash the place up," Jan finished. "It could only be you, Lily."

"I would have given anything to have seen the look on that PT's face when the kettle bell went sailing through the glass doors," Frankie said, then shrieked with laughter again.

Denise scolded them. "Now, that's enough. Lily could have seriously hurt herself." Denise seemed to have decided on sympathy rather than laughter, though her lips were twitching.

She turned to Lily. "I hope you've thrown that awful stuff out."

By "awful stuff" Lily assumed she meant the pre-workout powder, and she nodded. She had thrown it in the bin as soon as she'd been released from hospital, vowing to stay away from anything performance enhancing from now on. "I didn't mean to go overboard with it. I just thought I could do with the extra pep. Who even reads the instructions on stuff like that anyway?"

"Uh, everyone?" said Frankie, running her fingers through her dark bob. "That's what instructions are for."

Denise patted her hand. "Your willingness to experiment is what makes you a good chef, but maybe leave the improvisation in the kitchen next time, OK?"

"Fine. But how am I going to lose weight now? I'm back to square one. I can't go there."

They all laughed. "No, you certainly can't," said Lorna.

"Diet!" shouted Frankie.

"Exercise," added Jan.

"Oh, *very* helpful," snapped Lily. If all it took was diet and exercise wouldn't everyone be skinny? It was ridiculously hard not to put food in your mouth. When she got hungry her body sent all these signals to her brain. Like, *I will die if I don't eat all that bread right now.* And it was true. If she didn't eat she would die. But how could she communicate to her body that one piece of bread was enough, not four, with bacon? And fried egg. God, she was hungry right now and breakfast had only been an hour ago. She eyed the plate of biscuits on the table longingly.

It wasn't just the cravings, either. She worked hard, long hours and ate what and when she could.

Denise said in her most gentle, motherly voice, "Honestly, Lily. That is all it is. Diet and exercise. There's no quick fix."

Lily sighed. "I'll try. I really will. But you don't know what it's like working in a kitchen. We eat in between waves of customers, and it's hardly what you'd call diet food. It's good food."

Frankie adjusted her tiny bottom in super skinny jeans on the kitchen chair. "It's just self-discipline. It's easy."

As if you'd know, Lily thought, as Frankie had always been stick thin.

"Surely you get sick at the sight of all that food after a while?" Jan asked. "I know I would."

Lily stared at her. Sick of food? That was crazy talk.

Denise shook her head at Jan and Frankie. "You two don't know what it's like, you've been skinny all your lives." She turned to Lily. "Remember how big I was last year? Come to Waist Shedders with me. It's what helped me lose the weight after the girls were born."

Denise was a tall, hourglass-figured size 14 and looked fantastic. She'd looked fantastic as a size 18 after her two children as well. Lily would kill for her figure or any of her friends' figures in fact, but she wasn't built like they were. She was short and big-bummed, more pear than hourglass or stick. It wasn't as if they didn't put in the effort to look good but Lily felt deep down that they still had it easier than she did with their body types and having jobs that didn't revolve around food.

Waist Shedders was like AA for overweight people, wasn't it? It didn't seem like her sort of thing as she preferred to do things under her own steam, but she trusted Denise and Denise swore by it. "OK. I'm willing to try anything at this stage. Sign me up."

Denise beamed at her. "Wonderful. The next meeting is on Tuesday afternoon. I'll pick you up and we'll get you all weighed in and signed up then."

Lily cringed inwardly. Weighed in. She hadn't got on a set of scales in years and she wasn't really sure that she wanted to now.

"Don't drink the Kool-Aid," Frankie muttered into her mug of tea, and Denise shot her a dirty look.

"What does that mean?" Lily asked.

Frankie just shook her head innocently. "Nothing. You girls have fun."

The Waist Shedder meetings were held in the village hall. It was mostly women in their 30s and 40s but there were a few men as well. Lily recognised some of them and they greeted her with excitement bordering on mania. Lily was here! She had joined them! She was very, very welcome! Their effusiveness was a little alarming and she stuck close to Denise, wondering why everyone was being so strange.

"What's everyone so thrilled about?" Lily asked Denise out of the corner of her mouth after she'd been hugged by one of her parents' neighbours whom she'd never seen hug anyone in her life.

"It's a close-knit group," Denise whispered back. "They like new members because it motivates everyone. And don't look so afraid, for heaven's sake, they're just being friendly."

Many of the members hugged Denise too and complimented her on keeping the baby weight off. Apparently she'd stopped attending regularly since she'd reached her goal weight and a few of the women shot her an envious look, which they quickly covered with smiles.

A trim woman with a 100-watt smile stood at the front of the room as they all took their seats. "Hello, Shedders!" she trilled. "And how are we all this week?"

The group beamed back and said in unison, "Shaping up, Sharon!"

Lily felt her eyebrows creep up her forehead and took another furtive look around the room. Chanting together? This wasn't how people behaved in her village. Was this some sort of alternate dimension?

Sharon's smile got, if possible, even brighter. "That's what we like to hear. Whether you've lost, gained or maintained this week we're happy to have you, or have you back." Her smile landed fondly on Denise. Denise smiled back at her.

Then Sharon's gaze fell on Lily and she gasped in delight. "A new member! What's your name, dear?"

She was aware that everyone had swivelled to look at her and the back of her neck prickled. "Uh, Lily."

Sharon clasped her hands together. "Lily. What a pretty name. Welcome, Lily."

The group chorused at her, "Welcome, Lily!"

One after the other the members got up to be weighed in, something that took quite a lot of time because most had to be encouraged, cajoled and supported through the whole process, as if they were contemplating a bungie jump rather than stepping on scales. Sharon wrote their weight on a giant poster on the wall that tracked each members' progress down the weeks. Some people cried when they found they'd gained weight. Some cried when they'd lost it. There was lots of hugging and talking and exclaiming. Lily didn't begrudge anyone their emotions or tears because losing weight was a hard thing to do, but the level of emotion on public display was surprising to her.

She leaned over and whispered to Denise, "It's a bit cultish, isn't it?"

Denise's mouth flattened into a thin line. "I can't believe you let Frankie get to you with that Kool-Aid line."

Lily sat back in surprise. She hadn't even understood the Kool-Aid line. She got out her phone and surreptitiously texted Jan. *At Waist Shedders meeting. Said it felt a bit like a cult and Denise got all annoyed about that Kool-Aid comment of Frankie's but I don't get it??*

The reply came through straight away. *Drinking the Kool-*

Aid is a reference to a cult at Jonestown. They were all brainwashed into drinking poisoned Kool-Aid by the leader and died.

Ohhhhh. Ugh! Awful. Thx.

No wonder Denise had been annoyed by that comment, she loved Waist Shedders. Lily, though, probably wasn't going to. How could she be tactful about this?

But before she could figure out a way Sharon was motioning for Lily to come up to the front of the room to be weighed. Lily froze. Get on that scale in front of all these people and have her weight shouted out? Tell everyone just how much weight she wanted to lose and see their eyes slide over her, looking at all her bulges and rolls? Judge her? Talk about her later? She clamped her hands onto her chair. No way.

"I'm fine thanks," she called in a high voice.

"Don't be afraid," Denise urged her. "We're all friends here."

"We're all friends here!" Sharon sang out, beaming round at everyone, and Lily guessed this was a line that had been said a hundred times before to shy members. *We're all friends here!*

But Lily wasn't sure that she wanted to be a member and she didn't feel like any of them were her friends, except Denise, and Denise hadn't even got on the scales herself. "Honestly I'm fine."

But Sharon wasn't having it. She came down the rows of chairs toward Lily, giving off friendliness like a nuclear reactor gave off radiation. "Come along now, you'll feel much better once it's over, like ripping off a plaster."

Everyone nodded and smiled at her.

It is a cult, she thought in a panic. Lily leaned back in her seat, shaking her head. Maybe if it was just the girls she could do it, people who were actually her friends, but all this falseness wasn't working for her. She stood up quickly but instead of heading for the front of the room she bolted for the door, pushed through it and went out into the carpark.

Out on the gravel she came to a halt. She hadn't brought her car. She'd come with Denise. Well, she wasn't going back into the meeting. She'd just wait for Denise outside.

Denise appeared a few moments later, her mouth in an even thinner line, car keys in hand.

"Sorry," Lily mumbled as they both got into Denise's car. "I guess I panicked. I'm not used to being on show like that."

"It's fine. You've made your feelings perfectly clear."

But Lily could tell from Denise's tight face that it wasn't fine, and in fact she was very embarrassed. "I'm just not very good at group situations with strangers. Don't be mad at me, Denise, please. I'm not ready to deal with things like this."

Denise relented. "I'm not mad. I promise. Maybe it was a bit daunting. I forgot what my first meeting was like."

"Did you get on the scales?"

To Lily's surprise, Denise started to laugh. "I did, and then I burst into tears and sobbed all over Sharon. I was a complete mess but nobody laughed at me. I think that's why I love it so much, because they were all so kind to me that first day." She shot Lily a teasing look. "Even if it is a bit like a cult."

Lily grinned. "Just a little," and they both laughed.

"All right, so Waist Shedders isn't for you. How about we take beach walks down at Portrush every week instead then?"

Lily beamed at her. Portrush was a beautiful spot and the sandy beach below the cliffs was her favourite to walk along. Even on wintry days with the wind whipping around you it was beautiful and bracing, as long as you wrapped up warmly.

"Perfect. And can I still get your menu book? Even if I don't join Waist Shedders?"

Denise laughed and started the car. "Of course you can, as long as you cook my meals as well. No cult membership required."

After Denise had dropped her home Lily thought about it and decided she would join a new gym in the next village. It was a pain that she'd have to go several miles out of her way every time she wanted to exercise but this was her penance for being so daft about the pre-workout.

Feeling like she'd done something positive for herself at last, she found she was in a very good mood. As she leaned against the kitchen counter watching her mum prepare dinner she told her, "I'm going to lose at least two dress sizes by the time I go to Spain. I'm giving up fried food and sugar and carbs at dinner."

Mary nodded at the glass in Lily's hand. "And the wine?"

Lily made a horrified face and took another sip of her Sauvignon Blanc. It was her day off. She always had a glass or two of wine on her day off. "Give up wine? I might be on a diet but I'm not mad, mum. Anyway, it's got antioxidants."

Colleen was reading in the next room and called out, "Antioxidants are in red wine, not white wine. And I'll give you £50 if you can tell me what an antioxidant is."

Lily paused, glass at her lips, scrambling through her pop-science knowledge gleaned from glossy magazines. What even was an antioxidant and what was it for? "They prevent oxidants," she said confidently.

Colleen snorted.

"You can't tell me I'm wrong though, can you?" Lily called back, taking another sip from her wine. Nothing was going to kill her good mood today. Everything was back on track and she could practically feel the Spanish sunshine burnishing her future bikini-body. It was going to be wonderful. She was going to be wonderful.

CHAPTER EIGHT

Lily looked at the pair of jeans in the drawer. She took them out and held them up, examining them in the morning light. They were blue and skinny with a slight stretch to the fabric, but most importantly she hadn't fitted into them for the last three years. She'd stubbornly held onto them in the vain hope that she'd be able to wear them again because in her mind she was a skinny girl, really. This bum she had was only a temporary condition.

Plus the fact they'd been bloody expensive jeans.

It was five weeks since she'd started going to the gym regularly and watching what she ate. She hadn't been crazy-strict like Lorna was. Bread had passed her lips. There had been the occasional fried egg and bacon breakfast and several (more than several) glasses of wine some nights. But her clothes were feeling looser and she was feeling stronger and more svelte. Could she...?

There was only one way to find out.

She stepped into the jeans and pulled them up to her hips,

thinking *please please please* as she did up the button and fly.

And they fitted. Not in a stomach-squashing can't-sit-down way, but properly fitted, like she could go out for a meal in them. Turning this way and that in front of the mirror she admired how far she'd come in just a few weeks. Not just in relation to her figure, but also in that she no longer felt a deep sense of dread every time she left her parents' house to go to work or to meet her friends; dread that she would run into Mickey and Kiera. She still thought about them but it was more of a background trepidation than an all-consuming fear now. The village was small. It had to happen again eventually.

Unless they move to Belfast, Lily thought, looking at her rear end. *Or the moon.*

She took out her phone and snapped a few photos of herself, and she sent them to the girls with the caption, *Ladies. I am in my skinny jeans.*

The responses came back immediately.

Ayyyyyyyyyyyy mama! Lorna said.

Looking hot, babe, added Denise.

Frankie's message was longer. *You know what this means? Shopping trip. Time to get you a new wardrobe for Spain. Who's free to go into Belfast this weekend? Lily, you're off this Sunday, aren't you?*

Jan, Denise and Lorna were busy but Jenny came back with an enthusiastic *Yes!!*

Lily wrinkled her nose. *But I'm not at my goal weight,* she replied. She still wanted to lose at least another five pounds, and besides, she dreaded the thought of changing-room mirrors. They were always so unforgiving, showing you your arse from angles you'd rather not see. And what was it with the awful lighting that washed you out? It was like the shops wanted to make you feel dreadful. Did that really sell clothes?

Lily, do you have anything, ANYTHING remotely sexy to go with those skinny jeans you're wearing? A few tops and pairs of shoes will still fit you when you get a bit smaller. Handbags. Some accessories.

Whoa whoa whoa. Handbags and accessories too? Do you think I'm made of money?

You don't need to get everything at once. I'm thinking date-night outfit. You need to be prepared.

Lily scoffed at her phone. That was rich coming from Frankie, who hadn't been on a date in three years as men didn't complement her lifestyle. *I'm not dating anyone anytime soon. Nuh-uh. No way,* she replied.

Clothes are important, Lily. They can lift your whole mood.

The others chimed in their agreement.

Fine, Lily typed. *But I'm choosing what I buy. This isn't one of your style makeovers, Frankie.*

"We need to make over your whole style," Frankie announced as she parked her car outside the Belfast department store.

Lily groaned, her head falling back against the headrest. She'd feared exactly this when Frankie and Jenny had pulled up outside her house that morning to pick her up, an almost manic smile on Frankie's face. Shopping was her addiction.

"A few tops and shoes you said. I can't afford a Frankie makeover and I don't want one. I'm happy as I am."

Frankie held up her hands in mock surrender. "All right, all right. I'll settle for one top and one pair of shoes as long as they're the right sort."

Lily and Jenny exchanged knowing looks as they got out of the car. The *right sort* to Frankie meant designer brands.

Frankie put one manicured hand on Lily's shoulder. "Let me choose some things for you, Lily, please? If you don't like them you don't have to buy them."

Lily looked at her friend, fashionably dressed in a long, flowy kimono and patent pointy-toed high heels. She did look amazing. "Fine. But try and make them my style, not yours."

"Of course, darling!"

20 minutes later Lily was looking at herself in a black corset top and platform wedges. Her boobs were up around her ears and she wasn't entirely sure they weren't going to fall out. She opened the curtain with a snap. "No."

Frankie was crestfallen. "But Lily, you actually look like you have a bust in this."

Lily was aware that she didn't have much in that area but this top was putting just about every inch of her on display. "Where would I even wear this? I'd look like a hooker if I showed up in this on a date."

"Don't wear it on a date, then. Wear it because it makes you feel fantastic."

Jenny stood beside Lily and turned over the price tag. The

expression of horror on Jenny's face was all Lily needed to know. She marched back into the changing room and took it off. "I need practical clothes," she called through the curtain. "Things I can wear in the village, in Spain. Not hooker bustiers that cost as much as a week's rent."

Frankie took them to several more stores and had Lily try on a variety of clothes, some of which were better in terms of style but were still wildly expensive. Lily didn't need silk blouses and boucle blazers and expensive shoes. She needed fun, cheap clothes for the pub and the tapas bar. She came out of yet another changing room shaking her head, and Frankie looked like she was going to blow up.

Jenny stepped in. "Look, Frankie. Why don't we let Lily choose the store and then you give your opinion on what she chooses?"

That sounded like an excellent idea to Lily, and Frankie grudgingly agreed. They went into a jeans and summer dresses store that had university student prices and Lily began picking out things she liked, feeling in a better mood.

A mood that shattered as soon as she came out of the changing room in a yellow blouse and grey jeans. Frankie pinched the bridge of her nose. "No no no. Yellow, with your complexion? Really? You chose this godforsaken store, fine. Let me at least choose the clothes. Sit. Stay." She pointed to a couch like Lily was her misbehaving dog.

Lily, who was glad for the opportunity, sat down. She and Jenny slumped against each other.

"She goes a bit mad when she's shopping, doesn't she?" Jenny said as they watched Frankie flit about the store.

"As a hatter," agreed Lily as she offered her friend a piece of sugar-free gum.

A quarter of an hour later Frankie came back with an armload of clothes which she passed to the changing room attendant. "I don't hate these," she said to Lily. "Go try them on."

Lily ignored the attendant's offended expression and did as she was told. Despite feeling tired with the whole thing, she liked what Frankie had chosen. A maxi dress that didn't make her look shorter than she actually was. A long-sleeved, scoop neck lace top. Some slim-fitting embroidered trousers. As she came out to show each item off both Frankie and Jenny looked pleased. More importantly, Lily felt good in these clothes. Her body looked good.

"All right," she finally conceded to Frankie as she passed her chosen items to the cashier, "bringing you along wasn't so bad an idea after all."

Frankie looked smug. "It was an excellent idea and you know it. You're welcome."

"Time for lunch?" Jenny asked hopefully.

"God yes," Lily enthused. "Let's have a proper lunch. Something with menus and food I don't have to cook myself."

They chose an upscale burger and pizza restaurant and while they were waiting for their food Lily went to the restroom and changed into the new scoop-neck top. It went beautifully with her skinny jeans. Looking at herself in the mirror she felt like she was a whole person again for the first time since *the incident,* not just someone who was scratching to get through the days, hoping for the worst to be over. She was someone who could sit with her friends over lunch and enjoy herself.

When she got back to the table she saw that her smoked salmon salad had arrived, though she looked with envy at Jenny's burger and fries.

"Lily, you look lovely. I was always envious of your figure," Frankie said as she picked up her knife and fork.

Lily goggled at her. "Mine? But you've got legs for days."

"Yes, but I haven't got an arse to speak off. You know what they called me in school: Stick-figure Frankie. Men used to follow you down the street with their eyes, and they were doing that just now as you walked out of the bathroom. I might not want a boyfriend but that doesn't mean I don't want to be desired."

Jenny nodded, and winked at Lily. "You've got those curves that make people look twice. It's nice to see them on show again. Anyway, did you both hear about Denise's eldest's primary school teacher and the affair she's probably having with the principal?"

Jenny launched into the story of the affair and Lily listened happily while sneaking several of Jenny's chips to go with her salad. She had envious curves, did she? When was the last time anyone had complimented her on her figure? Mickey hadn't in years. When was the last time she'd noticed a man looking at her in an admiring way? It was a nice feeling, the thought that she might be desirable after all. A powerful feeling.

Jenny and Frankie were probably just trying to build up her confidence with their compliments but every now and then she glanced around the restaurant wondering if she really had been drawing eyes and, if so, who they belonged to.

As they were heading out to Frankie's car Jenny nudged her. "Isn't that Mickey's brother?"

Frankie gave her an outraged look and jerked her head at Lily, as if to say, *Could you be any less tactful?*

But it wasn't Alex she was afraid of seeing. Lily looked across the large shopping centre foyer and saw that it was him. He was too far away to speak to but he saw her at the same time her eyes landed on him and he stopped in his tracks, looking at her with a strange expression on his face. Half pleased, half wary. He was alone, and looked good in his jeans and a black shirt, his curls unruly. She noted again how he didn't resemble Mickey at all, which she was grateful for. He was broader, less polished, and with different angles to his face. Seeing Mickey's doppelganger around would be as bad as seeing Mickey himself.

Lily was painfully aware that they hadn't spoken since the afternoon he came in to repair the fuses at the restaurant. The night she and his brother had broken up. His loyalty would be to Mickey, of course, as family came first, and Lily felt a pang. She and Alex had never been super close but they'd always been friendly. One time when she was in high school and got sick at a friend's birthday party he'd given her a lift home in his car. Lily had unwisely drunk two huge glasses of very cheap, sweet wine and had thrown up in the bushes. Alex was 19 then and had been going out with the birthday girl's older sister. She'd been annoyed when he'd left her to take Lily home. Alex had shrugged it off as he'd driven her home, saying that being at a party when you really didn't want to be there wasn't fun at all.

Are you talking about me or you? she'd asked him, because he seemed happier as he drove her than he had been at the party. But he'd laughed and hadn't replied. He'd waited in the driveway until she'd got inside the house, too. He was thoughtful like that. Two days later she heard that he and the girl had broken up.

"Why is he never with a woman?" Jenny wondered out loud as she waved to him.

"Mickey always said that he's choosy and he likes his own company," Lily said.

Jenny turned to Frankie, eyes wide with delight. "He's like the male version of you. Oh my god, why don't we set the two of you up?"

Alex and Frankie together? Lily had a funny feeling in her chest, tight and resentful. "Don't be stupid, Jenny. That would never work."

Jenny deflated a little. "Why not? You can't deny that they've got things in common."

They did have things in common, but Lily still didn't like

the idea of her tall, attractive friend being interested in her ex's brother. *It's because he's my ex's brother,* she thought. *It would be weird because of that.*

Lily was saved from trying to put her dislike of the idea into words by Frankie herself. "Oh, please," Frankie said, giving Alex a cursory wave and hustling the other two in the direction of her car. "He's so homespun and he never has an opinion about anything. And besides, *if* I ever date it will be someone with a personality very different to mine. That's meant to be the secret of a good relationship: not having too much in common."

Privately, Lily didn't think 'homespun' was a bad thing, though she wouldn't use that word. He was a warm person, someone with a good heart. And she suspected he did have opinions, a lot of them, but he was the sort of man to keep them to himself.

Lily found herself glancing back as they walked to the car, wondering if Alex had noticed that she looked different, and if his eyes had followed her curves as she walked away.

CHAPTER NINE

"This looks amazing, Mrs Keane, thank you so much," Jenny enthused, digging into her lasagne. She, Lorna, Denise, Jan, Frankie and Lily were all clustered around Lily's family dinner table, along with Mary and Lily's Nanna Maureen. Colleen, Andrew and Rob were out. It was girls' night, and the wine was flowing from several open white wine bottles.

"Well I'm glad someone's eating," Mary chided, looking at everyone's half empty plates. Lorna only had salad on hers.

Denise took a piece of garlic bread from the plate at the centre of the table. "It's the holiday, Mrs Keane. We're all thinking of our bikinis. Just one piece of garlic bread for me. Can't hurt," she said, biting into it with relish.

Lily looked on enviously. She didn't dare have any bread as the morsel of pasta on her place was more than her usual carb allowance already. It had taken a lot of self-control, a lot of salad and a lot of workout sessions, but she'd lost two whole dress sizes since sending the kettle weight through the glass doors of the gym. Once she was in Spain she could let herself off the leash a bit, because what was a holiday in Spain without a whole lot of cheese, fresh bread and wine? And then she could work it off on the dancefloor.

Spain. She felt a warm glow at the thought. They'd be there in just a few days, soaking up the sun, relaxing on the beach and eating whatever they wanted, because they'd dance it all off again at night.

"You're all beautiful as you are, girls," Mary said, lovingly putting a hefty slice of lasagne onto Lorna's plate. Lorna's eyes widened in horror and she stared at the food like it was going to leap up and shove itself into her mouth.

"In my day," Maureen said, accepting a top-up of her wine from Jan who was seated next to her, "we'd eat nothing but cabbage soup for a week if we wanted to lose weight."

Lily had seen photographs of her nan when she was a young woman and she'd been a stunner. Petite and slim with dark hair and thick lashes. She'd always liked to dress up and look fashionable and that habit continued. There was a silk scarf knotted around her neck and she wore earrings that matched her bracelet. When the girls came over or she found them all in the pub Maureen could gossip just as well as the rest of them.

"Did that diet work?" asked Jenny.

Maureen shook her head. "Lord, no. We'd bloat like balloons and fart non-stop."

Mary sighed, exasperated. "Mum, not while we're eating, please."

The others were all shrieking with laughter, and Denise was nodding. "That was me on my brassica diet right after I had my first baby. Nothing but cauliflower, cabbage and broccoli for four days straight. My husband wouldn't come near me."

Jan tried to refill Frankie's wine glass but Frankie covered her glass with her hand and wrinkled her nose. "Not that one," she said, looking at the Chardonnay bottle in Jan's hand. "It's cheap and nasty."

Jan rolled her eyes. "God, you're such a princess. Can I have the Chenin Blanc down near you Lily? Her highness doesn't want the Chardonnay."

Frankie shrugged an elegant shoulder. "I know what I like, is that so bad?"

Lily grinned and passed the Chenin Blanc down to Jan. She'd been looking forward to this night all week, a chance for her and all the girls to sit down and discuss their holiday. They'd booked their flights two weeks ago and confirmed the house booking and that there were six people coming, not two. They were flying out in three days' time and had 10 whole days in Spain. Lily hadn't had such a long holiday in years.

There were four bedrooms, and it was decided that as it was her holiday Lily would get first pick and have a room to herself, someone else would take a room to themselves and the other four would share, two to a room.

But the question was, who was going to get the room to themselves and who was going to share with who?

Mary got up from the table as the girls squabbled over

the solo room, went to the pantry and came back snapping a piece of spaghetti. "Here. Whoever gets the shortest piece gets a room to herself."

The girls all drew 'straws'. Jan got the smallest piece of spaghetti and held it aloft. "Yes! That room's mine."

"I'm not sharing with Frankie," Lorna said immediately. "Jenny, you share with Frankie. You seem to be able to put up with her moods."

Denise nodded. "Yes, I'll share with you, Lorna. I don't want to share with Frankie either."

Frankie looked supremely unconcerned by this, as if her reputation for being difficult didn't bother her one bit.

Jenny cast her eyes to the ceiling. "Fine. I guess this means I won't have to put up with Lorna having sex in the bed next to me at least."

Denise went white. "Oh god. I never thought of that. Can I change rooms?"

"No!" chorused everyone at the table, while Lorna spluttered in outrage.

"Fuck you all, you're just jealous I can pull!"

"Have you all packed your condoms?" Maureen asked them, and then winked at Lily.

Condoms. Lily hadn't thought about condoms in years. She was on the pill and had forgotten that any sex in her future was going to involve a little foil packet. Would she even remember how to put one on a man?

"Mum, please," Mary said, frowning down at her dinner.

"What?" Maureen said airily. "Lily, Lorna, Jenny and Frankie are all single and they're on holiday. I'd be packing condoms if I was going."

"Mum."

To the girls' delight, Maureen went on. "Well, I would. Your father wouldn't have wanted me to be a nun. I've half a mind to come with you to Spain and show you girls how it's done. I fancy a Spanish man." Mary tried to take the wine glass from Maureen's hand but she moved it out of her reach. "Not that there's anything wrong with our local lads. That Billy Shepard is a handsome one."

"Lorna had him at New Year's," Jenny told her with a sly smile.

"I had a *kiss*, thank you," Lorna interjected. "Just a kiss. And maybe a grope of his arse," she couldn't resist adding to squeals and laughter.

Maureen leaned forward, eager. "Well, how was he?"

Lorna shook her head. "Sloppy. That's why it stopped at a kiss, Maureen."

Maureen nodded. "Wise girl. If they can't kiss then they'll be even worse with their pecker. Now, Spanish men. Spanish men are said to be wonderful lovers. And they age so well."

"You should come along, Maureen," Denise told her. "We'll get you set up with someone dark and hunky."

Maureen nodded, her cheek flushed with wine and the idea of hunky Spanish men. "I should my dear, I should. Show you young things how it's done."

"Mum, this is Lily's holiday. Stop trying to muscle in."

Lily grinned at Maureen. "You'd be welcome to my Spanish hunk, Nanna. I'm right off men."

Half the table made shocked noises. Lorna spluttered, scandalised, "If we don't get you kissed by at least three Spanish men then what even is the point of this whole adventure?"

The point to Lily was to relax in the sun with her friends, not stress out about men and how attractive or otherwise she might be to them. She'd reached her goal weight last week and was feeling good about herself, but the thought of another man, even one who looked like a swarthy Spanish prince, left her feeling anxious. Had she lost her mojo? Maureen, nearly three times her age and post-menopausal, seemed to have more go than Lily did. "Three? Lorna I'm not you," Lily spluttered.

"Fine," Lorna said. "One then. I'll take the other two. But we're not leaving Spain until you've blown off some of those cobwebs from certain areas." Lorna gestured at Lily's lap with her knife and Denise and Jenny snorted with laughter.

"Cobwebs! I do not have cobwebs down there," Lily protested. "And I thought we were talking about kisses, not... *that*. And we'll see about the kisses," she added quickly, and her mother nodded approvingly. Lily couldn't help but wonder about her mojo even more if she'd got to the stage where her mother was approving her decisions.

"Speaking of having a clear out," Denise said, taking a second piece of garlic bread, "have you all booked in to have your waxes and tannings done?"

Frankie and Lorna started regaling the table with the numerous treatments and bookings they'd made at the nearby salon. Lily vaguely listened while she tried to picture dark-haired, brown-eyed Spanish men with five o'clock shadows. They all looked handsome enough in her mind but none of them were setting off tingles…down there. Besides, there were dark-haired, brown-eyed men in Ireland. What was so exotic about Spanish men? Irish men were pretty damn good-looking. One in particular sprang to Lily's mind, the tousle-haired Alex as she'd seen him in Belfast while she was shopping with Jenny and Frankie. Now, he was a good-looking man, and you didn't need to go all the way to Spain to—

She cut off that thought in horror wondering where it came from. Did thinking about Alex mean she missed Mickey? She didn't want to miss Mickey and she didn't want to think about him, either. At all. It was bad enough knowing that she might run into him at any moment when she was out in the village but so far, she'd been lucky. Alex wasn't like Mickey in looks or temperament but he was his brother and that was too close for comfort.

Even if he was very good-looking.

"How about you, Lily?"

Lily came back into herself with a start of surprise and found they were all looking at her. She felt herself flush bright red. Did they know who she was thinking about? Had she accidentally said his name out loud? Were they all mind-readers suddenly? "Me? Me what?"

"Your treatments before the holiday?" Frankie prompted.

Lily slumped in relief. Oh, that. "I'll just run a razor over my legs or something the night before."

Lorna looked doubtful. "But what about your bikini line? I'm not sitting around the pool with you while your hairy bits poke out all over the place."

Lily choked on her sip of wine. Since when was this dinner table talk? *God, I really am turning in to my mum. Better watch out for that.* "I'll run a razor over that too."

The girls all winced. "You can't do that," Frankie told her. "Razor burn. It'll ruin your holiday. You need to get professionally waxed."

Let someone get up close and personal with that area? No way. "I don't need a beautician to take care of a bit of hair. I'll manage it."

"Listen to your friends," Maureen urged. "You don't want a thicket of weeds between your legs when you come face-to-whatsit with a nice Spanish man."

Mary rolled her eyes while the others giggled. Lily grinned at her. Nanna had always had some out-there opinions.

"It's best to leave it to a professional, Lily," Jan said. Jan spent half her pay-check on treatments at this time of year, getting ready for the wedding and party season. Lily wasn't used to that sort of extravagance.

"It's not just the waxing," added Lorna. "There's your hair, spray tan and nails to think of."

"They sell hair dye, wax and fake tan at the supermarket. It's fine. I'll do it myself. I like doing things myself."

Frankie raised her perfectly threaded eyebrows. "Jesus, this is going to be a disaster."

Denise shot her a look. "Don't be so negative, Frankie." But she turned to Lily and added, "Are you sure? You're not exactly...experienced at this sort of thing."

Lily refilled her wine glass, feeling confident that she was doing things the smart way. She didn't have time for a lot of bookings. "I'll take care of it. Don't worry. Mum, did you say there was chocolate cake for dessert? I think I can sneak in a tiny, tiny piece. This is a treat night after all."

The others were still looking at her doubtfully as they cleared their plates away and accepted various sized servings of chocolate cake, but Lily didn't let them rattle her. People did their own beauty treatments every day. How hard could it be?

The next day after her shift Lily gazed at the array of waxing products in the chemist, bewildered. Why couldn't they just make one sort? Even the same brand seemed to have five different items to choose from. Hot wax. Wax strips. Wax for the legs. Wax for the face. Wax for sensitive skin. Did she have sensitive skin? Lily had no idea. Finally, she saw them: wax strips for the bikini line. There were three different brands and she couldn't tell the difference so in the end she picked the cheapest. Before she went to the register she chose a shade of chestnut hair dye, some pale pink nail polish and a bottle of fake tan. Sorted, and in under 10 minutes.

Who needs professionals? she thought as she handed over her card. Lily was doing this the smart way.

When she got home she had a large glass of wine while she went through her social media, and then she poured herself another and took it into the bathroom she shared with Colleen. May as well enjoy a bit of pampering and pretend it was a posh spa treatment she was giving herself.

Besides, the wine would take the edge off ripping the hair from her sensitive bits.

When Lily had moved back in her sister had dutifully—if sulkily—moved her things to one side of the bathroom shelves, but since then Collen's cosmetics and hair products had crept slowly onto Lily's side. Part of it was probably that Lily didn't have much to fill the shelves with apart from a toothbrush, a hairbrush and some supermarket face cleanser. Defiantly, she put her purchases on the shelves, shoving Colleen's back. She could have plenty of girly products, too.

Sipping her wine, her eyes grazed the instructions on the box of wax strips. *Place over desired area...rub firmly...pull off in opposite direction of hair growth...*yada yada. Easy. Honestly, the way the girls were going on about it last night Lily would think that waxing your bits was like trying to fly to the moon. It was just hair.

But when she dropped her pants and regarded her lower half in all its untamed glory she felt a moment's pause. She'd never been one for fussing over her lady garden and during the winter she'd just let everything grow out. Where to start when there was so much to deal with? Feed it or weed it?

Then again, wasn't there something on the packet about the strips only working when you had hair to put them on? That would mean they would just work extra well for her. The strips themselves were on flexible cloth with a paper wrapper over the wax. She peeled one apart and sniffed. It smelled faintly of honeydew melon. Her coochie was going to smell fantastic—not that there was anyone to smell it, and not that she even wanted anyone in that general area right now. Her mind turned back to the thought of handsome dark Spanish men. And then to Alex.

Alex. Why was she thinking about him again? Was it her brain's way of telling her she missed Mickey? But she didn't feel sad when she thought about Alex as she did when she thought about Mickey. God, her brain was being so weird.

"Focus on the job at hand," Lily muttered, taking a swig out of her wine glass and then ripping the rest of the wrapper from the wax strip. She stood, legs akimbo, and began slapping the strips onto her bikini line and between her thighs. She put some between her bum cheeks for good measure as well. Best to have it all off at once. A few minutes later she was coated with the strips. They really had been generous with the number of strips in the box. This was turning out to be very economical.

Her phone buzzed and she saw that the girls were blowing up the group chat so she sat down on the loo to read, glass of wine in hand.

LOCAL LILY GOES TO SPAIN

Jan: *Would it be bad of me to bring a suitcase? I can't fit everything into a cabin bag*

Jenny: *Yeah but you'll have to pay for stowed luggage*

Frankie: *Are you kidding? It's 10 days, I'm taking a suitcase and I've already paid the charge. We're going to need at least three outfits a day, you know.*

Jenny: *Three?? Are you insane???? And can't we just all take a cabin bag, I hate waiting at those luggage carousels*

Lorna: *Watch out Jenny you're starting to sound like Frankie. I hate this. I hate that.*

Frankie: *Ha ha. I'm taking a suitcase and three outfits a day is perfectly reasonable: one outfit for the day, one for the pool or beach and one for the evening. And matching shoes*

Jan: *Same tho. OK Frankie I'm taking a suitcase too*

Lorna: *We can see you lurking Lily. What are you bringing?*

Lily grinned, because she would be showing as online at the top of the chat. She put down her wine so she could type. *I guess a suitcase but I don't have much to put in it. I plan on wearing a sarong over my bikini 80% of the time. Maybe put on a pair of flip-flops for evening wear.*

Lily anticipated a wave of outraged messages from Jan and Frankie and they arrived a few seconds later. *No flip-flops when we're not at the beach!!!*

Lily: *I'm kidding I'm kidding.*

Sort of. She did plan on making an effort in the evenings when they went dancing but honestly? By day three even Jan and Frankie would have given up on the fashion parade. Jan would pull her long hair into a high ponytail and would be reading a fat romance novel by the pool, and Frankie would have dark glasses on over her un-mascara'd eyes while she browsed fashion magazines.

Lorna: *We can swim at the pool AND the beach, god I'm so excited. Don't forget to pack runners, I want beach-running companions*

Frankie: *Everyone remember to bring a bottle of gradual tan so you can top up your fake tan each night before you go to bed. You're not stealing mine. It's expensive*

Jenny: *Oh my god. Who's going to remember to do that?*

Frankie: *I'm going to do that and so should you if you want your tan to last*

Lily laughed. Frankie sounded so firm about it now but by the fourth day even she would be too lazy or hungover to apply her gradual tan before bedtime. Lily re-crossed her legs and felt a tug, and then remembered the wax strips swathing her bits and thighs. They should be good and melted in by now and easy to pull off.

She stood and pulled up the corner of one. Grasping it firmly she took a deep breath—and pulled. She shrieked in pain and hobbled about the bathroom, trying to walk it off. She was having a bit of trouble walking, though.

Oh, god.

Her thighs were stuck together.

A voice called out from the next room. "Lily? Are you all right in there?"

CHAPTER TEN

"I'm fine," Lily said through gritted teeth. The last thing she needed was Colleen barging in here.

"You don't sound fine."

"I said I'm fine."

There was the sound of retreating footsteps and a muttered, "OK, OK."

Lily looked down and assessed the situation. The strip had seemed to work to some extent as it had pulled some of her hair out, but it hadn't come off as she'd hoped it would.

"Oh, god." She tried to cut the loose bit of strip with nail scissors but they wouldn't go through the wax.

A hot shower. That would melt everything away. She turned the shower on the hottest she could bear and stood under it for several minutes. Then she tried tugging at the strip again. It wouldn't budge and it *hurt*. She reached round behind her to pull at the strips at the back but they were stuck fast, too. She couldn't open her legs now. She couldn't even go to the loo if she needed to. *Shit shit shit.* This wasn't going as planned. Not at *all* as planned.

Lily looked around the bathroom desperately, hoping for inspiration to strike. Her eyes landed on her phone and she snatched it up.

It was close to midnight and she prayed Lorna would still be awake. A moment later she answered. "Lorna?" she whispered down the phone. "I've waxed my bum cheeks together."

There was a moment's stunned silence. "You've *what*?"

Lily explained what had happened with the strips, her legs being stuck together, the nail scissors and hot shower over the noise of Lorna screeching with laughter.

"Lorna it's not funny!" she hissed.

"Yes, it is. It's hysterical. Oh my god, this is the pre-workout all over again. When are you going to learn to read instructions? What was that last part again? I missed it."

"Because you were laughing too loudly!"

"I wasn't laughing too loudly, you're talking too quietly. Why are you talking so quietly?"

"I'm at my parents', remember? I don't need everyone knowing about this. What do I do?" she asked urgently.

"What sort of strips are you using? Are they wax or are they a fruit gel?"

"I don't know! They're waxy but they smell like fruit. What the hell have I bought, some sort of wax–fruit hybrid? Are they ever going to come off? *Lorna, I can't pee.*"

Lorna stifled another bout of giggling. "Calm down, it sounds like wax. You can get it off easily. What you're going to do is go down to the kitchen and get some olive oil and then you're going to rub it in at the edges of the wax and work it loose."

Down to the kitchen? She wasn't sure how she'd get down there but that wasn't her most urgent thought right at that moment. "Will the oil dissolve the wax?" Lily asked hopefully.

"Of course it won't," Lorna said scornfully. "Don't pour the oil on and then start yanking, you'll only hurt yourself. You're going to rub the oil in and then carefully pull it back. OK?"

When she got off the phone Lily knew a moment of despair. She was going to have to ask for help. Inwardly groaning she opened the bathroom door a crack.

"Colleen?" she called in a wavering voice. "Can you do something for me? If you laugh I swear to God I will murder you."

Colleen's face appeared at her bedroom door, piqued with interest. "Oh, yes?"

It was several hours before Lily was finally free of the wax. She worked at it with the olive oil that Colleen had brought up to her and a pair of nail scissors to cut away the hair. To her credit Colleen hadn't laughed—not until Lily had the bottle in her hand and had closed the bathroom door again. Then she was sure she heard Colleen stifle some giggles.

It was awkward work. Lily would never have guessed how hard it was to peel wax from your own arse. She hoped she'd never have to use this information again as long as she lived. She wouldn't wish this on her worst enemy.

Well. Maybe on Kiera fucking McCrary.

It was the early hours of the morning when her nether region was finally free and Lily slumped down onto the loo seat, panting and exhausted. Hairy wax strips littered the bathroom floor and her bits were an oily, ragged, red mess.

But at least she could pee.

Lily topped up her wine glass, took a fortifying drink, and texted Lorna. *All right you win. I'll come with you to your beauty appointments.*

Lorna didn't reply, but then it was nearly two in the morning. After finishing her glass of wine and cleaning up the strips, Lily went to bed.

"There! Tidied you right up." The beautician beamed at Lily's underpants area and liberally sprinkled her with talc. Lily looked down and saw with shock that just about every hair which had survived her disastrous waxing attempt of the night before had been ripped out by the roots. She was left with just a thin stripe right down the middle. Like she was a racing car. Or a badger. So much for a 'bikini' wax. She could get away with a piece of string if all she wanted to cover was the hair that was left.

The beautician saw Lily's horrified expression. "I had to take everything, love, you'd made a right mess of yourself. And besides," she added, giving Lily a wink, "something to surprise your holiday fling with."

Lorna was in the next room over, separated by only a partition, and had been loudly regaling the women working on her and Lily's nethers with tales about their holiday and how she was going to have at least three holiday flings and that Lily was certainly having one, too.

As Lily was pulling her jeans back up Lorna opened her cubicle door and beamed at her. "There, now, don't you feel better?"

"I feel cold," Lily said, wrapping her arms around herself. And she felt...bald. Like a baby mouse. Was it sexy, though? She and Mickey had never discussed pruning each other's underpants areas and he was more or less it when it came to her experience with men. *Who cares what Mickey thinks, though?* she thought defiantly.

Lorna beckoned her. "Don't be silly. Now, manicure for you and spray tan for me."

Lorna and the manicurist discussed what would best suit Lily, tossing around words like 'gel nails' and 'acrylics' and all manner of things that Lily had never heard of. The manicurist got to work, clipping and buffing and gluing. She quickly lost interest and used her free hand to scroll through her phone. The weather forecast for Alicante that week was beautiful...

"There, all done," the manicurist said proudly.

Lily stared at her nails, her eye slowly widening. She hadn't been paying attention to what was happening to her fingers and now it hit home.

LOCAL LILY GOES TO SPAIN

The woman seemed perplexed. "Something wrong?"

Her hands looked beautiful, moisturised and supple as well as neat and elegant with the long, false nails with a French polish. She'd never seen her hands look so nice. Or so impossibly wrong for her job.

"I've just realised something." She couldn't go into work with these, she'd never be able to hold a knife properly. She held her hands out to the manicurist. "They're lovely. But please take them off."

When Lorna came back the manicurist was painting Lily's own small, short nails a pale pink. "What happened? Where are the acrylics?"

Lily shook her head. "Lorna, I've still got two shifts at the restaurant. I can't work in nails like that."

Lorna looked disappointed, but she brightened considerably when Lily told her how good her spray tan looked. And it did. Lorna was bright and glowing and would look perfect on a beach in Spain.

They paid and the beautician turned to Lily and said, "And we'll see you tomorrow afternoon for your hair and tanning, Lily."

As Lily walked out to her car she felt a slink in her step. There was a secret in her pants and despite her protests that she wasn't going to have any sort of fling on this holiday, the excited thought bounced around in her head: *What if she did?*

At four pm on Friday afternoon Lily was feeling fabulous. Her skin was glowing golden, her hair was a lustrous, shiny brown and was hanging down her back in waves. Her lips were painted with a new gloss she'd bought at the salon and she'd put on eyeshadow and liner as well as mascara. She took a turn in front of her mirror in her sundress and for the first time in months didn't pick apart her appearance or list everything that she wanted to change about herself. This was the Lily who was going to Spain and she was pretty damn proud of her. She'd worked hard for her.

Lily nodded at her reflection. "Not bad, girl. Not bad at all."

Her dad helped walk her case down to the pub and she kissed him outside the door. She'd decided to take a suitcase after all even though she certainly didn't plan on changing three times a day.

"You have a wonderful time," he said with a smile. "You deserve it after all, well."

After Mickey. This was the holiday he was supposed to be going on, too, but she couldn't regret that he wouldn't be there. She had her girls and that was far better.

Smiling, Lily hugged him. It had meant a lot to her that he and her mum had taken her in again after she and Mickey had broken up, and that they didn't mind that she was taking his holiday that they'd paid for.

There were a handful of people in the pub and she caught sight of Jan and Jenny out of the corner of her eye. She was about to turn toward them when she noticed someone else. Two people, in fact.

You've got to be kidding me.

It was Mickey, sitting up at the side of the bar facing her, drinking a pint with Alex. The two brothers stared at her, faces blank with surprise. Then Mickey looked away quickly, pretending not to have seen her. Alex continued to stare but Lily barely saw him. She was too aware of her ex-boyfriend. Why did he have to be here, today, ruining everything?

Pull yourself together, girl. You look fantastic. This is a good thing for him to see me like this.

Straightening, she shook out her hair, squared her shoulders and went over to the girls. She greeted them loudly. Lorna was at the bar, turned and saw Lily, and added to the drink order. A moment later she brought her a gin and tonic.

"Thanks," Lily gasped, taking a large sip. "Do I look OK?"

"You look amazing," Lorna assured her, and the others agreed.

They all grinned, delighted for her, and Lily felt a little better.

A few minutes later Denise and Frankie arrived and all six of them in the little bar were beginning to make a stir among the locals. A few of the regulars called out to them, asking what the party was about.

"We're off to Spain!" Jan called back happily.

The others echoed "We're going to Spain!" and all of them including Lily cheered and clinked glasses. She couldn't help the self-conscious prickle down the back of her neck as she did so and she took another long pull at her drink. Some of her anxiety began to ebb. They were in the same room and

128

nothing terrible was happening. It would be all right.

"He can't keep his eyes off you," whispered Jenny, her eyes bright.

Lily made a face. "Don't look at him, I don't care."

"No, not Mickey. Al—"

"Cab's here!" Denise called out, hurrying back over to them.

In less than 30 minutes they were at the airport and they all had another drink in the bar. Lily was feeling giddy with power. This holiday was the best possible thing that could happen to her. Then they decided to get a bottle of champagne, and then another.

Before she knew it, they were boarding. Lily sat between Lorna and Frankie on the plane, with Denise, Jan and Jenny in the seats next to them. Once they were in the air they all bought two white wines each in tiny bottles. They didn't even need to keep their giggling and chatter down because just about everyone else on the plane was drinking, too. They were all heading off on holiday and there was a festive atmosphere to the cabin.

Lily finished her two wines and ordered two more. She was just getting stuck into her fourth when Denise leaned across Jan to speak to her.

"Lily, don't you think you should slow down a bit? One in the air is worth three on the ground."

But Lily didn't want to slow down and that was just a silly myth. She was having too much fun, and she was on holiday.

"I'm fine! Cheers Denise for your concern, but I'm fine!"

"OK," Denise said, doubtfully.

Lorna toasted her, and they got into a deep discussion about the merits of Brazilian waxes, and then Lorna regaled them all—and several other rows of the plane—with the story of Lily calling her in a panic because she'd waxed her bum cheeks together. To her surprise Lily didn't even feel embarrassed and called out her own additions to the story while the others cackled with glee.

When the plane started its descent, her head started to spin. She closed her eyes and leaned her head back, wondering why she felt so strange all of a sudden. She hadn't drunk that much.

On her other side, she heard Frankie say, "Lily? Are you all right?"

Lily woke gradually, but not pleasantly. As she rose through consciousness the pounding in her head amplified. When she opened her eyes, she saw she was in a strange bed in a strange house. *Where am I?*

Oh. Spain. Jesus, she could barely remember the plane ride let alone arriving at the airport or the drive to the villa. Had she been...? Oh, god. She vaguely remembered being wheeled off the plane in a wheelchair. How many more drinks had she had after she'd told Denise she was fine? At least two. Maybe three. It was all Mickey's fault. Why did he have to be at the bar with his stupid face and reminding her of his stupid horrible cheating?

One of the girls must have put her to bed as she was wearing her pjs. Judging from the fact that yesterday's clothes were folded neatly atop her suitcase she guessed it was Denise.

As she walked out into the living room in search of some water and aspirin a cheer went up. Everyone was awake and eating toast and drinking coffee, though no one had bothered to get dressed yet. Frankie was in a short silk dressing gown and Jenny had on pj pants with clocks on them and a camisole that read 'Just Five More Minutes.'

"Look who emerges at last," said Jan with a smirk. She was sitting in front of a mirror on a stand and working her long honey-blonde hair into a complicated fishtail braid. Everyone looked stupidly fresh and happy, Lily thought resentfully. It wasn't fair.

She collapsed at the counter, her head sinking into her arms. Not only was she hungover but she felt guilty for getting so drunk that the others had had to take care of her. "I feel like shit. Did I act like a complete arse last night?"

Lorna snorted. "Don't worry about it, love. A perfectly normal reaction to running into your ex-boyfriend, if you ask me."

The others agreed. Jenny passed her a mug of coffee and Lily drank it gratefully. "You guys are the best. Oh god, this coffee is heaven sent."

Frankie sniffed her mug and wrinkled her nose. "This coffee is disgusting. When can we go into town for an espresso?"

Denise pushed the sugar over to her. "Soon, princess,

soon."

While the others waited their turn for the toaster or wandered in and out of the bathroom Lily dug her phone out of her pocket to check her social media. There was a text message on her phone and she had to look twice at the sender before it made any sense to her.

"Alex?" she muttered, frowning as she opened the message.

Did you arrive safely? You looked great. Sorry I didn't get a chance to speak to you.

Panic gripped her. Oh god, had she been plastered at the bar as well? Had she made a fool of herself in front of Mickey? She scrambled to remember. But no, she'd only had the two drinks at the bar. The carnage had happened on the plane.

Jenny leaned over her shoulder to read the message. "Oh, how nice of him," she said, and smirked at Lorna, who smirked back.

"What's that supposed to mean?" Lily looked between them, confused. It was nice of him but why were they acting like that?

Lorna looked innocent. "Nothing. Drink your coffee, we've got a lot to do today. Project Lily Holiday Fling begins now."

CHAPTER ELEVEN

"I'm coming, I'm coming," Lily called, hurrying out of her bedroom in black wedge shoes and a red sun dress. It had got dark half an hour ago but it was still so warm out that she didn't need a jacket or a scarf. "But I'm not drinking tonight."

The girls were all gathered in the living room, applying lipstick in the mirror, having pre-dinner wines and checking their phones. A groan went up at Lily's announcement.

"Coward!" Jan called from the couch, toasting her with her wine glass.

Jenny tossed her lipstick into her handbag. "Lily, it's the only true way to get over a hangover. Get right back on the horse."

But Lily breezed past Frankie and the offered glass of Chardonnay. The memory—or lack of, rather—of all those wines on the planes was too recent. She'd spent the day lying out by the pool feeling very sorry for herself, drinking glasses of warm lemonade and groaning. The sun and fresh air had done her some good and a dip in the cool water late in the afternoon had freshened her up. She'd bobbed about in the water, looking at the huge azure sky and the palm fronds overhead, while smelling the sea air. Mostly she'd marvelled at the sky. In Northern Ireland sometimes, you forgot that the sky could be that blue.

Now it was evening and they were heading out to dinner, one of the local restaurants Lily had looked up online and chosen. It had a reputation for excellent local food and a beautiful garden location. She wanted to be able to appreciate it which meant laying off the wine.

It was nearly nine o'clock before everyone could be wrangled into clothes and shoes and out the door, but that didn't matter in Spain where eating was always done late. As they strolled through the town Lily saw that it was beginning to come alive, tourists and locals slowly filling up the tapas bars and walking along eating ice cream.

The restaurant wasn't far, though Frankie had already started complaining that her stiletto heels were giving her blisters after just two blocks.

"Why did you wear such silly shoes, then?" Denise scolded. She'd become even more of a mum than usual, telling everyone there was a washing up schedule and a grocery shopping master list and taking control of the house keys.

"Silly? Excuse me but these shoes are extremely expensive and beautiful, *not* silly."

When they found the restaurant they all enthused at how

beautiful it was, with white columns and an open courtyard. The head waiter came toward them, menus in hand, and Lorna perked up.

"Ooh, el maître is hot."

Lily took a close look at him as he led them to their table. He was tall and lean in his white shirt and black pants, and his body beneath his clothes looked muscular and graceful. *As if he knows how to salsa*, Lily thought appreciatively, glancing at his shapely rear end. His forearms and throat were tanned as though he spent a lot of time in the sun.

"It's so nice to be in a restaurant and not have to cook," Lily said as she took her seat.

The waiter overheard. "*Señorita* is a chef?"

Lily hadn't realised he was standing so close. "Oh, ah—yes."

He beamed at her, his eyes a sparkling brown, and placed a menu into her hands. "*Muy bien*, I'll have the chance to show you the excellent food from our region. We are very proud of it. My name is Federico, and you must tell me if you need anything at all."

The others hid their smiles behind their menus or nudged each other, not very subtly. Next to her, Lorna looked like she was going to explode with excitement. "Flirt with him," she hissed out of the corner of her mouth, not very quietly.

Lily felt her face go red. Federico definitely heard that, but his smile didn't change. She could only hope his English wasn't as good as it seemed to be.

"Um, thanks."

Top-notch flirting, she thought, as Lorna cast her an exasperated look.

He moved on around the table, handing out menus and talking through the specials. Lily followed him with her eyes. He was gorgeous and he loved food. Who was this Latin god and could he be interested in her? Maybe a holiday fling wasn't such a bad idea after all. Even just a kiss from him would set her up for the whole year.

"*Grazia, grazia,*" Lorna was saying airily to the waiter as he left them to look at the menus. Then she rounded on Lily. "You have to sleep with him. He was all over you."

Lily looked desperately around for wine but they hadn't ordered any yet. So much for not drinking tonight. "He was not *all over me.*"

Jan nodded, her eyes sparkling brighter than her jewellery. "He did seem interested, didn't he? You could be in there, Lil."

"He was being polite to me because that's his job," Lily insisted. "It helps him get a bigger tip if he's nice to the customers."

He came back to take their drinks order and they all descended into rapt school-girl silence, punctuated by giggles. The consensus, to a woman, was sangria, lots of it, and quickly. When he came back to the table holding two huge jugs of iced sangria filled with fruit they all cheered, and he smiled around at them. His smile lingered longest on Lily. As soon as he'd poured out their drinks and was gone they all leaned in to discuss his hotness, the attention he'd paid to Lily and how they were all going to manoeuvre him and Lily together. Possibilities from giving him her number to "accidentally" spilling sangria on her dress so he'd have to sponge her down were floated.

"I'm *not* doing that," Lily said immediately as the others screeched with glee.

"This place becomes a salsa club after dinner is finished, doesn't it? Maybe he stays to dance with his favourite customers," Lorna said.

It did become a salsa club and a very popular one, too. "He looks like he'd be nice to dance with," Lily conceded, watching him pass among the tables of the restaurant. He moved very gracefully.

"And kiss?" Jenny asked eagerly.

"And kiss," Lily said finally, before burying her face in her glass again. The others whooped loudly.

"He's probably fantastic in bed, Lily, don't give up that chance if it comes along," Denise told her.

"Yeah, and you know what your nan said: if you've waxed it you might as well use it," Lorna added.

They were all howling with laughter as he came back to the table and Lily hoped silently, yet again, that he didn't understand every detail of what they were saying. Even though they hadn't ordered yet he began placing sharing plates of food in the middle of the table.

"The chef was so pleased to hear one of his colleagues was in the restaurant that he's insisted you try his signature dishes."

Lily gazed at each of the plates in turn as the waiter explained them. There were ox cheeks slow-cooked in dark sherry on a bed of soft polenta; fried squid with garlic aioli; patatas bravas; and ham and manchego croquettes.

"There's not too much onion, is there?" Frankie asked anxiously, a hand to her throat as she looked at the food as if it was about to leap up and attack her.

"Not at all, *señorita*, but if it is not to your taste I can bring you anything that you prefer."

And under the force of his handsome smile, even Frankie melted. "Oh, thank you so much. *Grazia*."

When he left them and they began to eat Lily let out a groan of pleasure. The food was divine. The others all stopped their furious matchmaking as they ate, passing around dishes and exclaiming over the tastes. The waiter came back a few minutes later to check on them, and was greeted with enthusiastic declarations of how good the food was from all quarters.

"If you would like, *señoritas*, for your main course I recommend the sharing steak with side dishes? It is the chef's speciality."

They all heartily agreed that the steak sounded wonderful.

"As long as it's not too heavy, Federico," Lorna said with a smile. "We plan on dancing after our dinner." He promised that it wouldn't be too heavy at all, and before he could leave she added, "And do you dance, Federico? I bet you dance beautifully."

He smiled round at them, his eyes landing on Lily. "Some nights I can be tempted."

The table dissolved in laughter as soon as they were alone again and Lily felt herself being elbowed from both sides.

"Yes, all *right*. Let me eat my dinner, will you?" But she was smiling as she said it and took another mouthful of the fruity sangria.

"Did you reply to Alex's text?" Lorna asked a moment later, again with that too-innocent expression on her face. Lily wished she'd stop doing that. It was as if she believed there was something going on with her and Alex, which was weird and gross considering she'd just broken up with his brother.

"Oh, no I forgot." She got out her phone and read his message again. *Did you arrive safely?* It was kind of him to check on her. She supposed he'd seen the look of horror on her face when she'd seen Mickey sitting at the bar and guessed she'd gone heavy on the wine after that.

Sorry for the late reply. Having a wonderful time and all are safe and well.

Lily sent the text off without a second thought and turned back to her plate. She was having too much fun here to think about home. After they finished their starters and ate their steak, they all refused dessert on account of dancing and went to the bar to wait for the dancing to get going. The sangria was going down beautifully as it was a hot night, and when the music started up the rhythm was so infectious that they couldn't help but start dancing.

Lorna had taken classes and began showing them the steps which they fumbled through, giggling and getting wrong. Several locals and a handful of adventurous tourists headed out into the courtyard, which had been cleared of tables

"*Muy bien*, you do not need my help at all."

They all looked round to see Federico smiling at them. He'd taken off his apron and changed into a shirt with a dark leafy print, looking more handsome than ever.

"Lily needs extra help," Lorna said, and shoved her toward him so hard she stumbled.

He caught her up in his arms. *Oh my god, it's like a movie,* she thought as she looked at him. He started to dance and she panicked.

"I don't actually know how to salsa dance."

He smiled at her. "Everyone knows how to salsa dance. I'll show you."

The steps were surprisingly easy once he'd taken her through them: step back, step together; step forward, step together. He took her hand. "And now spin." She spun and turned back to him with a breathless smile. "Perfecto. You are ready."

"No, wait!" she cried, but he took a firm grip of her hand and tugged her out onto the dancefloor. There were a lot of people there now so she didn't feel too self-conscious as she began to dance with him.

"Wow, some of these people are so good," she said enviously as she watched them.

"Not as good as you," he told her, which made her laugh. "I am serious. You have lovely rhythm." He raised her hand in his, a signal for her to twirl, so she did. When she came back to him he pulled her close, tight against his chest. He felt delicious against her, and the way he moved was heavenly. His mouth was close to hers, close enough to kiss. He was waiting for her, though, being a gentleman and not forcing the kiss upon her. All she had to do was tilt her mouth up to his. The music was weaving around her and there were stars in the sky overhead. It was perfect.

But she couldn't do it.

What's wrong with me? He's right there, waiting. I want to do it.

"I—" *I like you, Federico. Say that.* But those weren't the words that came out of her mouth. "I—have to go."

Immediately he released her and stepped back, though he looked disappointed. "It was wonderful dancing with you, ah?"

"Lily," she replied. Though what was the point of telling him her name now? She would never see him again. She felt the loss of his arms around her immediately and even through her confusion she was longing to say she changed her mind and that she wanted to dance some more. But he wanted to kiss her and that was suddenly so scary.

She turned and pushed her way through the crowd, berating

herself the whole way. *What's wrong with me? A gorgeous Spanish man is milliseconds away from kissing me and I panic?*

From the edge of the dancefloor she saw that Denise, Frankie and Jan were dancing together. Lorna and Jenny had found partners, Lorna with another tourist by the looks of it and Jenny with a local. Jenny looked so happy as she beamed up into the handsome face of an older Spaniard with a salt-and-pepper beard. They were standing very close, both of them clearly very relaxed and happy with each other. Lily felt a stab of envy. Why couldn't she relax like that? She thought about going over to Frankie and Jan but suddenly she didn't feel much like dancing anymore, and she hated the thought of seeing Federico dancing with someone else. All Lily wanted to do was go home. There was a pressure behind her eyes and in her throat like she was going to cry and she didn't know why.

She slipped through the crowd toward the door. The others were having such a good time. She would just ghost.

CHAPTER TWELVE

"What the hell happened to you last night?" Lorna's indignant voice reached Lily as soon as she stepped into the kitchen. Lily headed for the fridge and a glass of cold juice, not ready to face the others. The truth was she'd fallen into bed and cried until she'd fallen asleep and now she was too embarrassed to admit it. This was supposed to be a fun holiday, and a man had nearly kissed her and she'd wanted to cry. What was wrong with her?

"We thought you'd gone home with el hottie but then he told us you bailed on him!" Jenny said.

Denise took a long look at Lily, and then turned to Jenny. "What about you, Miss Jenny, and that man you were dancing with? He was old enough to be your father."

Lily shot Denise a grateful look as she poured some orange and mango juice into a glass. The others might be oblivious, but Denise always knew when something was wrong.

"He was not! Alonso is 43. My dad's 55." Jenny's smile

became dreamy. "Wasn't he handsome? He smelled amazing, too, and he was such a gentleman. And that *accent*."

Lily drank her juice, feeling vaguely wistful. Why couldn't she feel that way about Federico this morning, all gushy and excited? He was more gorgeous and gentlemanly than the man Jenny had been dancing with, and now that she thought of it he'd smelled amazing, too.

"Would you sleep with him though?" Jan asked, making a doubtful face.

Surprising everyone, Frankie said in a deadpan voice, "I would." They all rounded on her, staring, and she explained, "He looked rich."

They all shrieked with laughter and Lily finally felt cheerful enough to contribute to the conversation. "That's the ideal relationship for you Frankie: a sugar daddy. He spoils you rotten with designer labels and mini-breaks in his Mercedes and occasionally you deign to kiss his cheek."

Lorna shook her head. "He wouldn't be satisfied with a kiss on the cheek. You'd need to give him blow-jobs at least."

Jan made a horrified face. "But... that basically makes you a hooker."

"Certainly not," Frankie said, coolly. "It's just like any other relationship but with the expectations clearly defined. Women exchange their company for material goods all the time. Don't you accept presents from your husband, and doesn't he earn a lot more money than you?"

"Are you calling me a hooker?!" Jan spluttered.

Frankie took a long, pointed look at the diamond earrings in Jan's ears, the enormous engagement ring on her finger. "It's not like I wouldn't enjoy sleeping with a man like that. As long as I got what I was promised."

Lorna was weighing up the two arguments. "Jan has a partnership, not a financial arrangement. But I can see the merits of a rich man who wanted my company and wasn't too demanding about it, and spoiled me with all sorts of presents."

Denise grinned over her cup of coffee at them all. "Sounds like we should get you set up with a sugar-seeking-daddy profile, Lorna."

Jenny looked flabbergasted that talk of her handsome Spaniard had devolved into sugar daddies and hookers, and she struggled to take back control of the conversation. "Anyway, Alonso is gorgeous and I have his number. He could be my holiday fling. I don't mind that he's older. In fact, it's quite sexy."

Denise nodded. "Oh, hell yeah. Men like that get better with age. Like a fine vintage."

Jenny gave a little salsa boogie on the spot. "Good kisser, too."

Everyone turned back to Lily, whose heart sank. She wasn't out of trouble yet.

"And Federico?" Lorna asked.

"Federico what?" Lily poured out a mug of coffee for herself, avoiding everyone's gaze.

"Don't be thick. Was he a good kisser?"

Lily sighed. She was going to have to confess everything even though she still felt so stupid about it all. She pulled up a seat at the counter and sat down, wrapping her hands around her mug. "I don't know. We were having such a good time, dancing and laughing and talking, though his English isn't that great when he's not talking about food. He's so easy to be around. Didn't even mind when I stepped on his toes. And then..." They were all watching her expectantly. She gave a half-shrug. "Then he went to kiss me and I chickened out."

Lorna and Jan made a noise like the one Mickey used to make when Manchester United missed an easy goal, but Denise was looking at her shrewdly. "Are you OK, Lily?"

Maybe Denise could tell that her eyes were puffy. She shrugged. "Yeah, I'm fine. It was just weird. I don't know what came over me."

"Kissing someone else after a breakup is a big step. We should all—" Denise glared around at the girls "—go easy on Lily."

She smiled at Denise, grateful. She was feeling better. Silly talk with the girls always cheered her up. "I'm OK. Really. So, what's the plan for today?"

Lorna was dressed in yoga pants and a crop top showing off her toned midriff. She slapped a bottle of sunscreen and a bottle of water on the counter tap, smiling around at everyone. "Ladies, we are going on a hike. No excuses. Everyone finish your breakfast and change into your workout gear. Be ready to go in 15 minutes. It's time to work off all that wine we drank last night."

"But I danced it off," Frankie moaned. "And I have blisters."

"You danced off your starters, maybe. It's time to have a proper sweat. And Denise has plasters, don't you Denise?"

Lily headed for her room, taking her coffee mug with her. A long hike in the sunshine and fresh air sounded ideal.

Half an hour later they were all waiting out the front for Frankie, who hadn't yet appeared. Lorna was getting impatient, bouncing on the balls of her feet. Finally, she stood at the open front door and yelled into the house, "Oh my *god*, Frankie, will you *hurry up*."

A moment later Frankie emerged, scowling, a huge pair of sunglasses over her face and her body clad in new-looking and expensive workout gear. Her body didn't have any tone but she was thin enough for that not to matter very much. "If I get gangrene in my blisters it's your fault, Lorna."

"That's not a thing," Lorna shot back.

Frankie sniffed. "It might be."

"Come on, let's go," Lily said loudly, over the argument that was brewing between the two girls.

Lorna led them through the streets and up increasingly steep hills toward the mountain that loomed over the town. Frankie began to moan again when she realised that Lorna intended them to walk to the top along the zig-zagging walkway.

"Can't we just get a cab? There must be a road leading up."

As they climbed the town was falling away beneath them

with the ocean glittering beyond. Lorna told Frankie that it might be easier to get a cab to the top but she wouldn't get the same sense of achievement.

Three-quarters of the way along the path they stopped for a breather and to drink some water. They were all sweating and panting, and Lily, who'd been feeling fit after all her gym sessions, realised she wasn't quite as fit as she'd imagined.

They set off again, Jenny texting furiously as she walked.

"Who are you talking to?" Jan asked her.

"Alonso." Jenny smiled slyly. "He's very chatty this morning."

"Are you sexting?" Lorna grabbed the phone from her and read, "'I want to lick every inch of your body until you're crying out with need for me.' Oh my god, Jenny!"

They all shrieked with laughter and Jenny grabbed her phone back, though she didn't seem mad. "Let me reply already, we were just getting to the good bit."

As they walked along the girls all called out suggestions for dirty text messages. "Take me now, you Spanish stallion," suggested Denise.

"I want you now, Daddy Alonso," added Lorna.

"Would you stop it with the daddy thing? He's only 18 years older than me."

Lorna looked mischievous. "Fine. How about 'Ayyyy papi you're so big'?"

At the top of the mountain they all appreciated the view of the town below and the glittering blue sea stretching out beyond. It was a beautiful sight, and as the breeze blew over them, cooling their bodies, Lily took deep a lungful of air, finally relaxing.

"Look, there's our villa," Jan said, pointing out the roof and swimming pool far below them.

The walk down was a lot easier than the walk up and when they got home they all changed into bikinis and fell into the pool. It was a quiet afternoon of reading and dozing and making ham and manchego sandwiches.

At five, Denise glanced at her phone. "Ladies, it's wine o'clock."

The sun was still high in the sky and Lorna had a better idea than drinking by the pool. "Let's take our wine down to the beach and have a swim."

They put the bottles and plastic cups into a cool-bag with a tray of ice cubes, grabbed their towels and headed out the door. *It's happening already*, Lily thought with a grin as she looked around at her friends. Only day three and they'd all stopped bothering to dress up, walking through the streets in bikinis and cover-ups, slip-on shoes and messy ponytails. Even Frankie looked laid back and didn't have a lick of makeup on her face.

The beach was broad and sandy and filled with people sprawled on towels and under umbrellas. They headed for an empty spot along the sand, admiring the waves and the tanned bodies leaping through.

"Lily!"

Lily turned her head at the sound of her name spoken in an accented voice, and saw Federico walking towards her across the sand in swimming shorts and a short-sleeved shirt open down the front. She swallowed at the sight of him. He was as gorgeous in broad daylight as he was at night, with abs that belonged on a professional.

"You've come down for a swim? Would you all like to join me and my friends?" He pointed toward a group of tanned, good-looking young men who were sprawled on towels in the sunshine drinking bottled beer.

Lorna's eyes widened at the sight of them. "Oh, we'd love to," she said, before Lily could reply. She marched over to the best-looking friend and plopped herself down.

Lily smiled at Federico. "Don't mind her, she makes herself right at home." She and the others followed Federico to meet his friends. All the young men were waiters and chefs from local restaurants and seemed delighted that Federico had presented them with a group of women to talk to, and they were all made very welcome. As the girls passed out their cups of wine the young men, in halting English told them where they worked and the best things to do in town.

Jenny was still texting while she absent-mindedly drank her wine. She looked up at their host. "Federico, do you mind if I invite someone to join us? I met him at the restaurant last night."

Federico smiled, as if he knew exactly who Jenny was talking about. "*Si,* of course, your friend is very welcome."

Jan looked worried. "Jenny are you sure he's going to fit in here? You know, because he's so old?"

Jenny just poked her tongue out at Jan and kept typing. Shortly afterwards, Alonso came strolling along the sand toward them, and Lily had to admit that he was very good-looking with his salty beard and stylish, expensive appearance.

Jenny jumped up to greet him. "Alonso, this is—"

But Alonso was already shaking hands with Federico and greeting him like a friend. "I know Federico well," he said in an easy manner. "I am one of his best customers, you see?"

Jan leaned toward Lily and Denise. "Lily you should ask Federico how often Alonso does this cradle-snatching thing. I bet it's every week."

Denise wasn't having it and rounded on her with a hiss. "Jan, you just shut your mouth. You're salty because you're not allowed to flirt with any of these gorgeous men. Stop trying to ruin Jenny's fun, it's just a fling."

Jan took out her phone and subsided into sulky silence.

"Not that being married is going to stop me from flexing my flirting muscle," Denise told Lily with a devilish smile, and turned to the man next to her.

They were all too busy drinking and talking to swim, and soon the sun was slipping over the horizon.

Federico turned to her. "Would you like to have dinner with me?" Lily glanced at the others. "Well, you see, I'm here with my friends…"

Lorna jumped in quickly. "We were just going to lay low

tonight. Not do much. You should go have fun."

Denise glanced at Jenny, who was practically sitting in Alonso's lap. "I think a private dinner is what these two are planning on doing anyway." In a low whisper she added, "Go on, go and do something to make us married ones jealous."

Lily grinned at her. "All right. Maybe I will." As she stood up, brushing the sand from her legs, she said to Federico, "Should I go home and change, or...?"

Federico buttoned up his shirt and she was sorry to see the flat expanse of his belly and his muscular chest disappear. "No need at all, we are perfectly dressed for the places I will take you."

They walked along the beach and up a side street to a tiny tapas bar she doubted she would have found without a local's help. The food was heavenly, and Federico chose a Rioja that went perfectly with the small, tasty dishes.

He's seducing me with good food and wine, Lily thought as he fed her an olive. *And I don't mind one bit.*

They finished their glasses of wine and Federico announced he was taking her to the next bar. He paid and they left, but before they could cross the road he took her hand and tugged her into a doorway alcove. Her hands landed on his chest and she looked up at him, lips parted as he smiled down at her.

"You ran away last night, Cinderella," he said, teasing.

"Well, you know it was pumpkin time." But she smiled so he would know she was teasing too. He kissed her, and his mouth felt... Unfamiliar. But of course it was unfamiliar, she had never kissed him—or anyone other than Mickey in seven years. *Shut up and enjoy the kiss!* she told herself.

But then he was pulling away from her, holding onto her hand as they crossed the road, and she felt a thud of disappointment that she'd been too busy thinking to enjoy this gorgeous man kissing her.

I'm going to need a lot more wine.

They had it, more Rioja along with more food. The evening was warm and filled with music and Lily found herself sitting closer and closer to Federico, his hands on her thighs, her waist. He was easy to be with, talking her through the food of the region and funny little quirks of the Spanish language. Lily told him what "craic" and "codding about" meant - "you know, pulling a leg? Oh, you don't know what that is either?"—and he told her about *la caña*, which was "the cane" but meant an awesome person.

"There is also *comerse* which means 'to eat'. It is not slang but it has another meaning."

She looked at him curiously but his smile only widened. What else could it mean if not—oh. That sort of eat. She started to laugh, and he kissed her.

Well, he's made his hopes clear, she thought, wrapping her arms around his neck and kissing him back. She didn't remember deciding that she wanted to sleep with him but now that he was kissing her it seemed like a good idea. A very good idea. The best idea since the girls suggested they all come on this holiday.

She felt a momentary twinge of guilt as she left the restaurant hand in hand with Federico that she was abandoning the girls on their third night in Spain. But then, this was what they'd been hoping she'd do for months, find a delicious Spanish man to get Mickey out of her system. Suddenly Ireland felt very far away and she was intensely glad about that. She wondered what the others were doing at this precise moment as she was strolling her tipsy way with Federico through the streets. Maybe Jenny was doing the deed with her hot older man right now. There'd be some gossip flying around tomorrow.

But who cared about tomorrow. She was living her life now, in the moment, with Federico.

They reached his flat, a cute place in an old building, with high ceilings and an ancient wicker chair on the balcony. He explained that he shared it with two other waiters but they didn't seem to be home.

"So, we can be loud."

"Is that so?" she said with a smile. He pressed his hips tightly against her and she felt something jut against her hip. Lily's eyes widened. OK, wow, that was ... *unfamiliar*. She didn't want to compare everything to Mickey but the fact was she hadn't been around another man's anything in so many years and now it was right...there.

Well then do something with it, Lorna's snippy voice said in her mind.

All right, all right. She would do something with it. But first they needed to sort out a few details because even though her nan had told her to do it she hadn't put any condoms in her purse.

Nan, you'd be so disappointed in me right now. Her mum would probably be disappointed too, but for very different reasons.

Oh, god, why am I thinking about my family at a time like this?

"Condom?" Lily asked, and Federico frowned at the unfamiliar word. "You know, condom, for your…" she gestured vaguely at his crotch area but he still looked perplexed. Oh god, what was the Spanish word for condom? Lily looked at him helplessly, wondering how to mime 'condom' and wishing she'd just brought some with her. Maybe she should text Lorna to bring her some. But that was too embarrassing to contemplate.

Federico was looking at her like he had no idea what she was talking about. Fallen at the first hurdle. This was off to a good start.

CHAPTER THIRTEEN

So, this was what they called a walk of shame. Lily was doing it properly too, with yesterday's knickers balled up in her handbag, her sandals swinging from her fingers and her eyes squinting in the bright morning light. Somewhere between the beach and Federico's flat she'd lost her sunglasses.

As she turned into the street their villa was on she put her fingers to her lips and felt the prickle of beard rash. Federico hadn't shaved on his day off. With a grin, she remembered all his kisses of the night before. It was prickly but hell was it worth it.

She had hoped she'd be able to get into the house quietly but she didn't have the keys. Resigning herself to a confrontation with the girls, she knocked, and the door was yanked open a second later by a grinning Lorna. Lorna looked at her, and then called over her shoulder, "I win the bet! Lily's back first."

A cheer went up from the kitchen as Lily entered. Of course they would all be up, waiting for her to stagger in.

Lorna, Denise, Frankie and Jan were looking refreshed and neat, and presumably had had a good night's rest in their own beds and a hot shower. They were grinning at her, big, saucy grins like the one Lorna had given her. Lily had barely slept and she hadn't showered. She must look like something the cat had chewed up and left on the doorstep.

"Morning all. What's this bet?" Lily asked, accepting both a glass of juice and a mug of coffee from Denise, and perching at the kitchen counter.

"We had a bet going about who would get home first," Jan supplied. "You or Jenny."

Lily looked around the room. Where was Jenny? Then she remembered: Alonso. "Did she spend the night with her sugar daddy?" she asked with a grin.

Denise laughed. "You know it. After you went off with Federico, Alonso started dropping hints that he wanted to get Jenny alone but she pretended not to understand. Playing hard to get, you know."

Lorna shook her head, pleased and exasperated at the same time. "Honestly, she really put on a show and he lapped it up. It was perfect, because if there's one thing these older men love to do it's chase younger women. He was eating out of her hand."

They all turned gleeful, expectant faces on Lily and she knew what was about to happen. "Come on," Denise said. "Dish."

Lily took a sip of her coffee and pretended innocence.

"About what?"

"You *know* what."

She did know what. About last night, and sleeping with Federico. Lily smiled to herself. It had been, in a word, *fantástico*, once he'd figured out that Lily was asking if he had any condoms. Thankfully he had, and didn't have a problem with using one which she'd been relieved about as she'd heard horror stories about men who didn't think they needed to wear one. It had been a wonderful night...but that didn't mean she wanted to put a blow-by-blow account into words.

Probably didn't want to.

The girls started to laugh and she realised she was grinning like a cat who got the cream. "It was lovely. What more do you want to know?"

"Everything!" Jan exclaimed.

But just then the front door opened and Jenny strolled in, glowing and smiley, looking every inch the sun-kissed holiday belle. It was obvious that she'd had a very lovely night, too. "Hello, my dears," she called airily. "Did we all have a good evening?"

Frankie snorted. "Not as good as you, apparently."

Jenny shook her head at the offer of coffee. "No, thanks. Alonso took me to breakfast down on the beach, this very exclusive little hotel with fabulous coffee. We ate eggs royale. Simply divine."

Denise and Lorna's eyes were shining and Lily knew it was because they had two impending one-night-stand stories to feast on, not just one. Lily hadn't decided how much she was going to say but Jenny would spill the lot. If there was anything Jenny liked better than other people's gossip it was her own gossip.

"So, who's going first?" Lorna asked, beaming.

Jenny waved a magnanimous hand at Lily, clearly still floating on Alonso's attention and posh breakfasts. "You go first, Lily."

After they had figured out the condom thing and Lily saw there was one safely on the nightstand, she'd decided to tackle Federico's pants. But Federico had other ideas, namely, getting Lily's top off. It's was ridiculously easy to do as she was wearing a beach wrap and a bikini, both of which were only done up with bows. Two pulls on the strings and Lily was practically naked. He'd got her down on the bed and was sucking on her nipples before she knew what he was about, and a few seconds later she didn't much care as long as he didn't stop.

But how to put that into words for the girls? "He's... a good kisser."

The others exchanged looks. "I wasn't talking about that," Lorna asked. "I want to know about the rest."

Lily struggled not to smile at the memory of Federico edging down her bikini bottoms and then exclaiming over what he found when he'd got her naked. Or rather, what he didn't find. "He, ah, liked what the beautician had done. Down there."

"Where is it all? Were you robbed?" he'd asked with a smile up at her, meaning all her pubic hair, before getting to work with his tongue. The man could dance and the man could lick. She'd never felt anything so perfect in her life and she'd buried her hand in his hair and moaned with pleasure.

Denise grinned. "I'll bet he did. And did he give it proper attention?"

Oh, and then some. He made her come twice before even thinking about himself. Lily hid her face in her coffee cup, her cheeks glowing. "Yes. It was very nice."

Exasperated, Lorna turned to Jenny. "Jenny, give us the goods, please, and show Lily how it's done."

Jenny preened at getting the undivided attention of the room, scrunching her hand languorously through her hair. "Well, after we left you guys at the beach I insisted that Alonso drive me home so I could get changed. He planned on taking me somewhere posh and my sandy feet and salty hair weren't going to cut it. So, I had a shower and put on this long dark blue jersey dress and silver high heels. Thank god I had them with me." She spread her skirt and stuck out a leg, waggling her foot so they could all see her shoes.

Frankie nodded decisively. "Of course. You always need an expensive dinner dress on holiday, just in case."

"In case of sugar daddies," Denise teased. "Go on, Jenny."

Jenny was clearly warming up to her subject. "The restaurant he took me to was beautiful, at the top of some cliffs overlooking the ocean, and we had champagne and oysters, and then he ordered—"

Denise cut across her. "We're not interested in the food, get to the good stuff."

Jenny looked exasperated, but still pleased at all the attention. "*So impatient.* Well. As we were eating Alonso started to get a little handsy. We were in one of those little circular booths, you know? So we could sit close together and the long tablecloth hid our legs."

Lorna gave a delighted gasp, anticipating what was coming. "He *didn't?*"

"He tried," Jenny said with a grin. "But this is a very long dress so he had a hard time getting his hand up it, and I kept re-crossing my legs and scolding him for being so naughty."

And loving every second, Lily could tell by the look on Jenny's face.

"But he did get me all hot and bothered over dinner with all his whisperings and so on and it was such a long way back to his villa…"

Lorna's eyes had grown very large. "And?"

"And so, he took me back to his car and went down on me in the back seat."

Denise and Lorna shrieked with glee. Jan and Frankie clapped their hands over their mouths in delighted horror. Lily grinned, glad Jenny had such a good story to tell as it took the heat off her.

"What about the rest? After you got back to his villa?" Denise asked.

Here Jenny's smile vanished and she scrunched her nose. "Frankly, I was disappointed."

Lorna looked horrified. "Oh, *no*. Was he rubbish? Was it tiny?"

Jenny nodded sadly, holding up a thumb and forefinger. "Four and a half inches. Five if you were being really generous."

Taking another sip of coffee, Lily smiled to herself. Federico hadn't been lacking in that department at all. He'd started talking to her in Spanish as they'd done the deed, and she'd had no idea what he was saying but it was hot as hell. What was it about foreign men? She'd woken up this morning feeling supremely satisfied about the whole thing. Nothing about the night had made her feel weird or lonely or strange. Everything about Federico had made her feel wonderful.

Lorna looked hopefully at her. "How about Federico's?"

Lily merely took an ostentatious sip of her coffee and said nothing.

Her friend sighed, shaking her head. "You're no fun at all, Lily."

"Was it, you know, *girthy* at least?" Denise asked Jenny, making her thumb and forefinger into a circle and holding it up.

Jenny shook her head. "Underwhelming in that department too, I'm afraid. Still, he's good with his tongue and we can't have everything, can we?"

Lorna looked doubtful about that but didn't say anything. She had been dubbed, after showing so much interest in the size of every man's you-know-what in the village, the resident size queen. She had been at Lily for the longest time to spill the deets about Mickey's pecker but she'd refused. Boyfriends and husbands were off-limits when it came to Lorna's curiosity as far as Lily was concerned. They all knew Mitchell, Jan's husband, was well endowed, but only because he'd started out as a one-night stand and Jan had told them all about his goods, something she deeply regretted once she started dating him because Lorna took every opportunity to refer to Mitchell as 'Old Eight and a Half.'

To their surprise, Jenny stood up. "I can't sit around talking. Alonso wants to take me handbag shopping. He's picking me up in an hour."

Frankie looked sick with jealousy. "If he buys you Gucci or Dior I'll...I'll..." But it seemed she couldn't finish the thought and she pushed back from the counter with a noise of disgust.

As Jenny headed for the bathroom, Lily asked the others, "What did you all get up to?"

Denise sighed. "Oh, it was very dull. Frankie took us to a raw food restaurant where you couldn't even get a drink or a steak. It was so depressing we were all in bed by 10 and slept like the dead."

"Excuse me," protested Frankie, "it was delicious. And very good for you."

Lily drank down the rest of her juice and yawned. "Well, I'm heading to bed for a nap. I'll see you in a few hours." In the doorway to the kitchen she paused and looked over her shoulder. "Oh, and Lorna? Seven and a half."

Lorna looked perplexed. "Seven and a half what? Seven and a half *what*?"

As Lily was taking off her clothes in her bedroom she heard a screech from the kitchen through her closed door. "Oh my god! Federico!"

The phone was ringing and Lily picked it up without checking who the caller was. "Hmm? Hello?"

"Lily? Hi!"

The familiar voice seemed strange in the context of Spanish sunshine and Lily's brain was jammed like an old set of cogs. Who...? Then she realised who it was. "Alex! Hi?"

He made an uncertain noise and silence stretched on the line. Lily struggled into a sitting position. Why was he calling her? Had something happened? But what could possibly have happened that meant he would be calling her?

"I was just calling to see how you were?" he said, a little more uncertainly now.

"Sorry, I just woke up from a nap. My brain's being a bit slow. Lovely to hear from you."

He chuckled. "Big night last night?"

She felt her face flush red. There was no way in hell she was telling Alex that she went home with a Spanish man last night. "It was. We all went to the beach and drank a lot of wine. It went on quite late." A little white lie. He didn't need to know it wasn't with the girls. "How's things in the village?"

She lay down again on her back and listened to him talking

165

about the jobs he'd been doing and what was happening around the village. As the local electrician and regular visitor to the pub he knew everyone and everyone knew him. Everyone liked Alex, too, more than they did Mickey, now she came to think of it. Mickey could look down a little on local ways and local people, preferring to take his cues on what people were doing and liking in Belfast or other cities. But Alex loved the village.

It was relaxing hearing him talk, but he cut the call off soon after that, saying he'd kept her long enough. "Have a lovely time. Talk to you soon."

She frowned at her phone as she hung up. Alex had never called her just for a chat before.

As she was now awake Lily thought she'd go see what the others were up to. When she went out into the lounge room she saw there was a large paper shopping tote emblazoned with GUCCI. The girls were all standing watching Jenny as she posed with her new handbag, all admiring the beautiful brown and cream leather. Well, almost all. Frankie was scarlet with suppressed envy.

"Do you know how much one of these costs?" she asked in a choked voice, her fingers reaching out to but not quite touching the bag.

Jenny shrugged gaily. "No idea. It was Alonso's money."

The cogs seemed to be turning behind Frankie's eyes. "Maybe having a boyfriend wouldn't be such a bad thing after all. Where would I meet a man like Alonso back home? Maybe in Belfast? Or he could be a rich agricultural type who enjoys the finer things in life…"

"So, you wouldn't mind that he's only got a four-inch dick?" Denise asked. "You'd be all right with that long-term?"

"Four and a half," Jenny said quickly. "Nearly five."

"Oh, sorry," Denise said, trying not to laugh. "That extra half inch is so important."

Frankie was brought out of her train of thought and looked witheringly at Denise. "Why on earth are you talking about something so base as sex in front of this beautiful handbag? Can we not focus on what's important here?" She turned on her heels and went to her room.

Lorna snickered, watching her go. "That's the last we've seen of her all holiday. She's gone to bawl her eyes out over not having a rich boyfriend with a pecker like a baby carrot."

"*Hey*," said Jenny in a warning tone. "Frankie's right. Stop making such a big deal of his dick."

"Why not? I doubt anyone ever has before," Jan said, and she, Lorna and Denise broke down in peals of laughter.

They were wrong about Frankie disappearing in a sulk. A moment later she was back with her laptop and set up at the kitchen counter. Lily peered over her shoulder and saw that she'd typed "find sugar daddy Ireland" into Google.

"There must be a way," Frankie muttered to herself. A moment later she gasped in delight as a list of websites appeared, all with various combinations of "dating" "seeking" "sugar" and "daddy" in the URLs.

Lily looked on amused as Frankie started clicking through the websites, and then she turned to Denise and said, "Alex just called me. That's what woke me up. He just wanted to hear how I was. Isn't that silly?"

The only sound in the room was the clicking of Frankie's laptop mouse.

"Well...yeah," Denise said eventually. "He's liked you for ages. Since high school."

Lily stared at her, and then at the others. No one contradicted her. "What? No, he hasn't."

Lorna nodded. "Yes, he has. We thought you knew?"

Lily rounded on Jenny. "All the gossip you repeat—and repeat and repeat—and this is the piece you choose not to tell me?"

Jenny looked taken aback. "It's about you though! I just assumed you knew and that you went for Mickey over Alex, end of story. We all did."

This was all too much, seeing them take it all so calmly when she was utterly floored by the news. "So, all of you have been talking about this behind my back?"

Denise stepped in. "Lily, calm down. It's not like that. There was never ever a point where the five of us were all sitting around together talking about you choosing Mickey over Alex. It was just something we were all vaguely aware of, not something we furiously discussed."

Outrage was still coursing through her. Alex, like her, and not one of them mentioned anything to her? This was the sort of important thing that they shared with each other. "And none of you told me!"

Lorna pinched the bridge of her nose. "Lil, you're not listening to us. We didn't think we needed to tell you what seemed pretty obvious to the rest of us. We thought you knew. Don't you remember how you and Alex were in high school? Always teasing each other, being silly together, talking together. You got on better with him than you did with Mickey back then."

"Remember Michelle's party when you had boxed wine and got drunk?" Jan asked.

"Yes, of course I do," Lily snapped.

Jan looked at her expectantly, as if it was obvious what she was about to say. When Lily didn't cotton on she said, "It's not a coincidence that Alex broke up with Michelle's sister the very next day."

Lily felt strange all over. She had thought that was coincidence. "But nothing happened on that drive home. Are you saying that was my fault?"

"It's not your fault, it's not Alex's fault, it's not Michelle's sister's fault. It's just one of those things. Alex had probably been thinking that he liked his girlfriend just fine, but then seeing you again reminded him that he didn't like her that much after all. He liked you."

Lily slumped down onto the sofa, her head spinning. All the Christmases, birthday parties and nights at the pub she'd spent with Mickey as his girlfriend while Alex was there.

Had he been hurt to see her with his brother? But that was just getting ridiculous. She couldn't imagine some sort of heartbreak scenario where Alex had been pining away in silence for her the last seven years. That was preposterous. Wasn't it?

She got out her phone to look at his last message, needing to see if there was any subtext she'd missed, and saw there was another message from him, sent a few minutes after their phone call ended.

It's wonderful to hear you sounding so happy. You deserve a holiday after everything. It would be good to see you when you get back.

"Oh, my god," she said quietly. "It's true." She held up her phone for the others to read what he'd written.

The others read the message silently and then nodded. As Lorna was looking at the screen Lily's phone beeped. "Oh, you've got another message."

Lily half-expected to see Alex's name, but when she turned to look she saw Federico's. *Señorita, I would like to take you dancing again.*

Lorna looked at Lily doubtfully. "Do you…do you want to go dancing with Federico?"

She couldn't process this news right now. Alex having a crush on her for all these years and her being oblivious? It was too much. "A night of wine and dancing and forgetting all my problems? Of course I'm going. We're all bloody going!"

The relief that broke through the room was like a change

in the weather. Jan ran to the portable speaker to put some lively music on. Frankie peered into her phone, using the front camera as a mirror, saying she would have to do something about her terrible hair if they were going out in public.

Denise called out, "Lily, tell Federico to bring his friends so there are partners for all of us!"

Jan pretended to be scandalised about the idea of flirting again, but Lily could tell her heart wasn't in it. "Denise, we're *married*."

"So? You're only going to dance with them, not go to bed with them," Denise told her. "And tell Federico to warn them that we'll need a lot of coaching and will probably step all over their toes."

Jenny was texting, too, probably Alonso from the silly smile on her face.

Frankie, back at her laptop again, said to them all, "Help me choose a profile picture for this sugar website. Which one do you think makes me look the most spoilable? I think the right vibe to go for is sexy, vivacious and sort of disdainful. You know, 'I don't really need your money but whatever, I guess I'll take it.' Seeming too desperate is a huge turn-off. Men hate that."

"You look pretty disdainful in this one," Lorna said, pointing at a selfie where Frankie was all in black and pouting at the camera.

"But is it too disdainful?"

"That one," Denise said, pointing at a shot that showed a

lot of cleavage and highlighter on her cheekbones. "Men like boobs and sparkle."

From the other side of the counter Jenny made a little *"Hmmp!"* sound, and they all looked up at her. She was the only one not clustered around Frankie's laptop screen.

"What?" Frankie asked her.

Jenny shrugged, going through the lining and pockets of her new handbag. "Don't you think you're being rather greedy?"

"Oh?" Frankie said, looking between Jenny's face and Gucci bag. "Hark who's talking?"

Jenny scowled and stopped what she was doing. "I didn't start dancing with Alonso because I knew he was rich. I danced with him because he has a nice smile."

Frankie made a dismissive noise. "Please. You could tell he was rich just by looking at him. You knew what you were doing."

Behind Frankie, Lily exchanged looks with Denise and Lorna. Jan gave a little shake of her head, a *nope, I'm out* gesture, and went to go sit on the sofa. Something was brewing between Frankie and Jenny and it was going to erupt at any moment, and erupt big. Lorna tried to rescue the conversation by suggesting they all have a swim before the sun set, but Jenny didn't seem to hear.

"Why can't you let me just enjoy this? Why do you have to make it cheap and sordid?" There were tears glistening in her eyes.

"Girls, please." Denise walked around the counter and put

a placating hand on Jenny's shoulder. "There's no need to argue about this. You can both date men however you choose." But Jenny shrugged her off.

"Frankie always has to make things into a competition! Everything has to be about her! The food's not good enough for Frankie. Frankie's feet hurt. Frankie didn't meet the richest man on holiday so now she has to go on the internet and find one. Why can't I just have this one thing?"

Frankie was statue still and spoke icily. "I happen to like Gucci bags and you've hit upon a good way of getting them. I don't know why you're so upset. Imitation is flattery after all." Her eyes flicked over Jenny's denim shorts and frizzy hair, and she added under her breath, "It's not like I was going to copy anything else that you do."

"You're so full of shit, Frankie! You're not flattering me, you're making it gross." Jenny shrieked so loud that everyone winced. "Screw all of you! No one's on my side. I'm going home." She turned on her heel and fled to her bedroom, heaving with sobs as she went.

"Good riddance!" Frankie spat, and she picked up her laptop and stalked out to the pool. Two doors slammed, making the rest of them jump.

In the deafening silence that followed Lily stared around at Denise, Jan and Lorna, wondering what was going to happen now. Everything had been fine just moments ago and now their holiday was falling apart.

CHAPTER FOURTEEN

"Well, I'm still going dancing," Denise announced, "even if they want to sulk by themselves. A silly catfight over a handbag isn't ruining my holiday. I'm child-free and ready to cha-cha."

Jan agreed, and she and Denise went off to her room to decide what to wear. Lorna, who was in her running gear, took a swig from her amethyst water bottle and headed out for a jog.

Lily glanced at the time on her phone. Six-thirty. She'd have a shower and slap on some instant tan as she'd been too lazy before bed to apply any gradual tan. Then she'd do her makeup properly, using eyelash curlers, powder over her foundation, highlighter—the lot. Because that's what a woman did when she found herself pursued unexpectedly by two men at once: she maintained her hotness and put off making any decisions. It wasn't a night for introspection. It was a night for dancing. She went off to her room to gather her toiletries and pick her makeup. As she passed the door to Jenny's room she heard sobbing from within, and knocked tentatively.

"Are...are you OK, sweetie?"

Jenny's watery voice emanated from within. "Go away!"

Denise came up behind her and whispered, "Don't worry about her, I've seen this from my girls. Too much ice-cream, sunburn and fun and it all ends in a meltdown. A cry is the best thing for her, you'll see. I'll take some cucumber slices in for her eyes in about 10 minutes and have her fixed right up by the time we head out."

Lily smiled at her. "You're such a good person. You always know just what to do."

Denise shrugged complacently. "It's just practise. You'll be the same when you have bubs."

Bubs? A husband? Oh, god, she wasn't thinking about any of that. *Keep your mind on the salsa and nothing else,* she told herself.

An hour and a half later Lily, Jan and Lorna were gathered in the lounge, cracking open a bottle of white wine to share while they waited for the others.

"Do you think Jenny will really go home?" Jan asked.

"And miss all the fun? No, she was just being dramatic," said Lorna.

Lily wasn't so sure though. They hadn't heard Jenny crying, and Denise still hadn't appeared. Maybe she was still trying to talk Jenny into staying. And where was Frankie? There was no sign of her out by the pool.

They'd got halfway through their glasses of wine when Frankie appeared, composed and polished in a little black dress.

She accepted a glass of wine and said nothing about handbags or sugar daddies to the rest of them.

"I let Frankie use our room to get ready," Denise whispered to Lily. "You know, since she and Jenny are sharing."

She'd forgotten that those two were sharing. "And Jenny?" she whispered back.

Just then, Jenny entered the room, not with suitcase in hand but in a cocktail dress with her hair curled and wearing lots of black eyeliner. She held her chin aloft, unsmiling, and went to the fridge

"How are you feeling?" Jan asked her.

"Fine, thank you," Jenny said coolly, turning back to them with glass of wine in hand. "Do I have time to drink this before we head out?"

They all assured her that she did, there was no hurry. Personally, Lily felt that both Jenny and Frankie could do with at least two glasses each, and quickly, because they were still looking everywhere but at each other. She hated fights within their group. It made everything so awkward.

Denise stepped up to act as mediator, setting her glass of wine on the counter. "All right, listen up everyone. Now that we're all gathered together we're going to clear the air after this afternoon's argument so we can all have a good time tonight." She turned to Frankie. "Frankie, you were insensitive about setting up your sugar daddy profile right when Jenny was enjoying sharing her moment with Alonso." She turned to Jenny. "Jenny, you need to remember what makes someone special is how you feel about them and not what other people make of them and the presents they give you."

Jenny's jaw dropped open. "Is that all you're going to say to Frankie? That she was insensitive?"

Denise put up her hand. "Frankie pays her tax for making everything about her. No one wants to share a room with her. We all think she's a pain in the ass and occasionally say it to her face. Don't we, Frankie?"

Frankie nodded and gave an elegant shrug of one shoulder, a *what can you do?* gesture. "But you put up with me because you know I won't bullshit you about anything. The truth might sting but sometimes you need to hear it."

Jenny looked like she was about to start screaming again.

"We don't put up with you, *we love you*," said Lily. Then she caught the others' eyes. "All right, maybe we put up with you sometimes."

Denise nodded and added to Jenny, "You'll also notice that we can say this to Frankie's face and she doesn't get upset with us? She knows we sometimes think she's a pain in the arse but she's not about to change who she is to please us, and we respect that."

"Let me take this next bit," Lorna said to Denise, and turned to Jenny. "Do you think you were getting upset because you suddenly felt a bit slutty over the way you got your new handbag?"

Jenny thought about this, her jaw jutted angrily, like a toddler. "Maybe?" she admitted finally. Then she added, her voice more strident, "But I do really like him."

Lorna nodded sympathetically. "Of course you do. We all enjoy things in different ways. It doesn't mean that one person's way is right and another's is wrong. Frankie is unemotional about things. You're more of a romantic. Both ways are valid if they make you happy. You enjoy your present. We're all very jealous."

Being told that everyone was jealous seemed to placate Jenny. "Well, all right," Jenny sighed. She glanced at Frankie. "You are an arsehole sometimes. But I still love you. Friends?"

Frankie nodded decisively and held out her wine glass. "Friends. As if we were going to let a man come between us."

"Or a legion of sugar daddies," Denise added, grinning, and they all toasted to that and knocked back their wine.

"You know, that's probably one of your best qualities, Frankie," Lorna said shrewdly. "You never put men before your friends."

Frankie's eyes widened. "Well, why would I? None of them are worth it."

The conversation descended into telling each other what they valued about each other best, and it went from sincere to silly very quickly.

"Your boobs, Denise. I've always loved your boobs," Lorna said, waving a forefinger at Denise's chest.

"Frankie's got this look, like a duchess who could murder you for your bad manners by shooting lasers from her eyes. I've always wanted to be able to do that," said Jan.

"Lily's got this aura around her that makes people like her instinctively," Frankie said, looking at Lily like she was some sort of alien creature. "I have no idea how it works. Black magic, probably."

"Oh, stop it," Lily said, embarrassed. She also grinned, because Frankie not understanding how being pleasant and friendly worked was so very her.

Lorna nodded. "It's true. You're lovely and warm and you listen to everyone and always have time for people when they need you, and we're all lucky to have you as a friend."

To Lily's surprise the others all joined in on this, saying how lucky they felt, too, and how much they loved her. Lily hid her face in her glass of wine and told them to stop, because she wasn't used to people saying such nice things to her. And then she thought she was going to cry and looked imploringly at Denise to make everyone stop.

"I don't know why you're looking at me," Denise said, smiling. "If you're going to have a cry and ruin your makeup, go ahead. It's about time you cried some happy tears instead of sad ones."

Lorna wrapped her arm around Lily's shoulder. "Exactly. You deserve some happiness."

Lily sniffled, wiping her eyes and nodding. "All right, no more sad tears. Only happy ones." She looked round at all her beautiful friends and thought how grateful she was that they'd all come with her and made this holiday into a special adventure. She raised her glass. "To the best friends anyone could ever have."

The others hurried to refill their glasses, slopping some onto the counter in the process. "To best friends!" they all chorused.

Jan clapped her hands together. "All right, enough soppy stuff! I want to dance with these gorgeous young men that Federico has lined up for us."

Jenny was texting and looked up from her phone as they were all heading out the door. "Frankie might not want one of Federico's men."

Lily and Denise exchanged looks. Jenny wasn't about to restart the whole fight with a bitchy comment, was she?

"Oh?" Frankie asked, her eyes narrowed.

"No. Because Alonso's bringing his best friend for you to meet. His best friend who owns a yacht."

Frankie's face went blank with shock. "Jenny. That's the nicest thing anyone's ever done for me."

"We need a picture," Lorna screeched as they were walking along the street. "Make Alonso send you a picture of this man with a yacht!"

A few minutes later Jenny's phone beeped and she squealed and showed the screen to Frankie. They all clamoured to see and when the phone came to Lily she saw a handsome, fit man in his 40s holding a glass of wine on board a shiny white boat.

"If that's the standard of sugar daddies then I want one too," Lily joked.

Lorna took a closer look at him. "Look at the size of his hands! He's an eight-incher for sure."

Denise burst out laughing. "You can't tell. That is such a myth."

"It is not!" Lorna protested. "I've made a study of it. Good, square large hands mean you've got a quality package on your, ah, hands."

Lily overheard Frankie asking Jenny for more pictures of the yacht. "If it's a good pecker it's wasted on Frankie!" she crowed. "She cares more about his boat."

They all howled with laughter, except Frankie, who was too busy telling them all that they were terribly immature and that she cared about the important things in life.

"Do you think we can all go out on the yacht?" Jan was wondering out loud. "Think of the Instagram opportunities."

They reached the restaurant that Federico had invited them to. It was full but not unbearably so and the music wasn't too loud for them to talk. He greeted her with a broad smile, coming though the tables towards her, and her breath caught he was so handsome.

Federico kissed her on each cheek and turned to the others. "*Señoritas!* This way." He seemed to be in host mode even though he was off-duty, and led them over to a table where the young men from the beach were all seated, and Lily barely recognised them as they looked so polished in button up shirts and freshly shaven faces. Denise went straight over to the one she'd been talking to the previous night and sat down next to him with a flirty smile.

"I have arranged for a little cheese and wine tasting for us all," Federico explained, remaining standing while Lily and her friends sat down. "All local produce and all favourites of mine."

A waiter brought over some wooden boards covered in cheeses and placed them in the centre of the table, and Federico got to work uncorking several bottles of wine and pouring small measures into the bank of wine glasses on the table. Lily, Frankie and Jan listened closely as Federico explained which cheese went best with which wine and why, while Denise and Lorna giggled with the men they were talking with and drank the wine without bothering to taste it properly.

As Federico was standing next to her chair uncorking another bottle of wine, Lily looked up at him and said, "You did this for us? That's so kind of you."

Federico winked at her. "Don't tell the others, but I did it for you. Now, I want you to try this cheese. It's from a farm in a valley about 20 kilometres from here and you won't taste anything like it anywhere else.'

He leaned down and picked up a sliver of cheese, feeding Lily with his fingers. From the other side of the table, Lorna and Denise smirked at them.

Federico didn't notice. "I would like to own my own restaurant one day. Choose the food and wine. See people happy at the tables."

It was the very reason Lily loved being a chef, knowing

that the people just beyond the doors of the kitchen were having a wonderful time eating the food she and the others had prepared.

Once they'd finished eating the tables were all moved back and the DJ started playing salsa music. Federico was talking to one of his friends so Lily went to get the dancing starting with the girls, not minding being the first on the dancefloor tonight because who cared if she couldn't salsa like a pro? She was with her friends and that was all that mattered.

Frankie and Jenny were dancing together, one arm around each other's shoulders and laughing like the very best of friends. No one would have guessed they'd had a screaming fight just hours earlier, but that was the best thing about her friends. Even when they fought like cats they always made up, and their friendship was stronger than ever afterwards.

Lily was enjoying a dance with Denise when she spun and saw Federico behind her.

He held out a hand, large and warm, just like his smile. Just like how he made her feel when she looked at him. Federico was meant to be just a fling but was this how holiday flings were supposed to be? So happy and fizzy and romantic?

"Care to dance, *Señorita?*"

Lily reached out and put her hand in his. "Yes, I would. Very much."

184

CHAPTER FIFTEEN

L ily loved the pattern of their days in Spain. Long evenings of food and wine and dancing. Sleeping late and waking to full, hot sunshine. Swimming, hiking, shopping. More food. And then more dancing, often with Federico and his friends when they finished at the restaurant.

"I wish you could stay forever," Federico had murmured in her ear as they'd danced the previous night.

But it couldn't last forever even though Lily wanted to pretend it would. She was happy in Spain. He was just meant to be a holiday fling but she and Federico were getting along beautifully. They still confused each other talking sometimes despite his very good English. She didn't speak a word of Spanish, though he'd tried to teach her a few words when they were in bed together. The language they both spoke fluently was food and when he talked about opening his own restaurant one day she felt the excitement and possibility of a life in Spain.

Her happiness wasn't just because she was on holiday.

It was also because her home and all the painful memories that lived there were far away. What if when she returned they crept back into her heart? Sometimes she wondered if she'd be better off staying in Spain, away from all the pain back home.

Lily lay her magazine down in her lap and looked across the pool, thoughtful. Alex was there, too. Alex Kavanagh, tall and handsome, a good soul with a good heart.

And her ex's brother.

She sighed heavily and reached for her lemonade. How had everyone known how he felt except her? Would she have gone out with Mickey, had she known? She cast her mind back to being 17, and how head-over-heels happy she was when Mickey had been pursuing her. She'd grown to love him, and he had loved her, too. Once. She couldn't regret what they had had together, but she did wish it had ended a different way.

Two sunbeds over, Frankie let out a gasp and gripped the sides of her laptop. "Oh my *god*, guys. Look at this." She flipped the screen around and showed them all an electronic receipt for £800.

Lily didn't understand at first but on her other side Lorna flipped her sunglasses up and let out a cry. "Is that from a sugar daddy? Who? How? *Why?*"

Someone Frankie had never met had sent her £800? Lily couldn't believe it. For the last few days Frankie had been glued to her laptop, trawling sugar daddy dating sites, and then running off to her room to make phone calls.

"His name is Mason and he's a Harley Street physician. We've been video calling getting to know each other and he says he's going to fly me to London to have dinner with him next week. This is a little present to show he means business." The smile on Frankie's face was like a hundred-watt bulb. She rarely smiled like that, for anything, but it seemed that £800 did the trick.

Jenny hesitated. "It's not business, though. It's meant to be love."

Frankie waved her hand. "Stop imposing your out-dated courting rituals on this sort of relationship. It is business. I have monthly expenses and goals for the future. I've been reading up about this a lot and it's all about being supported and mentored by an older, rich man. And it says it right there in my profile, 'I'm looking for someone generous to help me to better myself through art and culture and learning foreign languages.'"

"But what does that mean really?"

"It means I have a need for designer handbags and top-shelf champagne."

Denise looked at her shrewdly. "Did you have to show him your tits to get that money?"

Frankie didn't look up from her laptop but she flushed. "Just one tit. Just a flash. Can't hurt to tease the goods."

They all squealed with laughter. So that was what Frankie had been doing when she ran off to have private phone calls in her bedroom. Lily wasn't above a bit of naughtiness on the phone, but she'd only done it with Mickey and after they'd been in a relationship for a while. She couldn't imagine flashing a bloke she barely knew.

"The goods? So, you have to sleep with him?" Lorna asked.

Frankie pursed her lips. "We'll see."

Lorna gave her a withering look. "Come on, Frankie. 'We'll see'? You know that in his mind sex is the end game. Neither you nor he wants you to feel like a hooker but he is paying you for your company."

"So what?" Frankie said hotly.

"So, a spade is a spade. Or in this case, it's a hooker."

Lily winced, fully expecting another screaming match to begin, but Frankie merely shrugged. "If you really want to go on about that, fine. But I just made £800 from a few phone calls, so…" She let her words trail off meaningfully.

Lorna and Denise exchanged looks, "Yeah. I guess you can't argue with that," Lorna conceded and put her head on her side, thinking. "Maybe I could even do it myself. How old is this Mason dude?"

"59."

Lorna shuddered. "I take that back."

After thinking for a moment, Denise said that she might be able to do it if she was really desperate for cash, but Lily shook her head. "Not me at all. It's not his age or him being a stranger. I can barely deal with the emotional turmoil of two men showing an interest in me. Add money for sex and being scrutinised by men old enough to be my grandfather, I'd go to pieces."

When Jan announced that she could do it, everyone stared at her. "What? I could. Not now that I'm married of course, but before I met Mitchell I used to meet with clients all the time and have to deal with old men looking at my chest and then trying to weasel out of paying me properly. I was very good at getting what I wanted out of them. This doesn't sound much different."

Frankie nodded. "Exactly. That's the way to think of it. Take the emotion out and think of it as business."

Lily didn't believe that the emotion *could* be taken out, not for her, but if Frankie was happy then that was all that mattered. They all subsided into thoughtful silence and Lily guessed they were all imagining this life of money for going on dates for themselves, but her mind strayed back to Federico and Alex. Things were complicated enough without imagining a whole other life for herself.

By her side, Jan heard Lily's regretful sigh. "I don't want to go home, either. I'm having too much fun. Can't we all just live here?"

"So tempting, right?" Lily agreed. The sun, the sea, the good food. People moved to Spain all the time to start new lives. Ireland wasn't that far away, really. A few hours on a plane was all it took to visit and flights weren't that expensive.

"We could all become professional salsa dancers in Federico's restaurant," Denise suggested. "Teach the tourists how it's done."

"He'd probably hire you if you asked. He wants to own a restaurant of his own," Lily said, turning a page of her magazine.

Jenny turned to look at her. "Oh? Have you two been talking about your futures together?"

"Not together. Just our futures and what we want from them. It came up while we were dancing," she said evasively, but the others seemed to be able to smell that there was something more to this. They all sat up, interested looks on their faces.

Oh, here we go. Can't we all go back to talking about Frankie and her sugar daddy?

Denise got straight to the point. "We've noticed that you and Federico get along really well for something that's just a holiday fling. Are you thinking of relocating to Spain?"

Playing for time, Lily took a sip of her lemonade. "No. Not really."

The others sat up even straighter, shocked and delighted at the same time, and Lily knew she'd said the wrong thing. She wasn't seriously thinking about anything, but lying in the sun in her bikini, who wouldn't be considering ways to extend this beautiful holiday?

She watched them all exchange significant looks, and then Jenny asked, "What about Alex though? Alex has loved you since you were teenagers."

"He doesn't *love* me," Lily protested. "He liked me back in high school, that's all."

Does he love me? Oh my god, maybe he's in love with me.

"He's never been in a relationship with anyone else though," Jan pointed out. "I think there are real feelings for you there. He's texting you now that you're single."

Denise nodded. "And he never texted you while you were with Mickey, did he? That means he's honourable. He respects the boundaries of a commitment."

Lily caught her unsaid meaning: unlike some people. Unlike his brother. It was a good sign, wasn't it? It showed that Alex was a good person as well as cute and local and dependable.

"But Federico is a whole new fresh start," countered Jenny. "There's too much emotional baggage with the Kavanagh boys."

Denise seemed to think it was time they all heard from Lily. "Go on, gun to your head, who would you choose: Alex or Federico?"

Who would she choose? On the one hand Alex meant local life, stability, familiarity. On the other, Federico was exotic and exciting. She loved the restaurant where she worked and having all her friends and family around her, but change could be wonderful, too. Look how much happier she was already after just this holiday. Maybe she needed an even bigger change. A life change.

"One of them is probably Mr Right," Jenny said eagerly.

"But which one?" Lorna mused. "The local lad we all know and love, or the exotic Spaniard who can show you a life of salsa and sun?"

"Alex!" Jan exclaimed. "Dependable, good Alex right there in our home village."

"Federico!" countered Denise. "Who needs dependable and local when you can have exciting and foreign?"

Lily shook her head, but she couldn't help smiling. Maybe they were correct and one of them really was her Mr Right. It was exciting to think so but she had to remain sensible. "Don't be silly," she demurred. "It's probably not even true about either of them really liking me. This is just holiday nonsense."

To distract herself from the conversation she looked at her phone and felt her mouth fall open. She had two text messages, one from each of the men.

Federico: *I am going to miss you bella. I wish there was some way I could see you again.*

Alex: *Can I see you when you get home? There's something I want to say to you.*

Jan was still talking about why Alex was clearly the right choice when Denise interrupted her. "What is it, Lily?"

She held up her phone so they could see the screen. "Oh my god, guys. I think you're right after all. It is a choice between Federico and Alex. They both like me. How can I possibly choose?"

Frankie was still reading her magazine, but she was shaking her head. Lorna noticed and said, waspishly, "Care to contribute? You obviously have an opinion."

"Of course she does," Jenny said, an undertone to her voice.

They obviously didn't think that Frankie's opinion counted for much when it came to relationships, and especially seeing as she'd taken to accepting money for dates.

But Lily turned to her, wondering what Frankie could possibly have to say about choosing between Alex and Federico. "Go on. I'm interested."

Frankie flipped the pages of her magazine. "You're all framing it as a choice between Federico and Alex and you're forgetting the obvious third choice."

"Third?" Lily squeaked. "Am I forgetting a man?" She scanned her memory but it had been just Federico she'd been kissing lately, hadn't it?

Jan looked at Frankie in horror. "You can't mean Mickey, can you?"

"Of *course* I don't mean Mickey. I mean that Lily doesn't actually have to choose between two men. She can choose no one and stay single and happy."

Denise made a dismissive gesture. "Well you would say that, wouldn't you? You don't believe in relationships."

Frankie slapped her magazine down in her lap. "No. I don't. But Lily does, and I am framing my opinion from her point of view. Lily has a tendency to jump into things feet first and you're all behind her trying to push her off the cliff. How about you just let her stand on dry land for a while?"

Lily felt her giddiness ebb away as she looked at the other woman. She was about to jump off a cliff? The others were trying to push her?

"Frankie," Denise scolded. "You're such a cow sometimes. Look at Lily's face. You've really upset her with your nonsense."

"I'm just trying to inject a little reality into the situation. Rebound relationships are cheap and nasty. You're above that, Lily."

"God, you're always so negative," Jan said. "How is it a rebound relationship when months and months have passed?"

Jenny turned to Lily. "Don't listen to her. You know how she gets. Doom and gloom about everything that doesn't have an expensive price tag attached."

But Frankie ignored the others and just addressed Lily. "Putting aside all this terrible encouragement the others have given you, you do have a tendency to jump first and ask questions later. What about the disaster with the waxing? The pre-workout? You don't stop to read the fine print."

The others snorted with outrage at this criticism and told Frankie to keep out of it, what did she know, Lily was *fine*. But Frankie was right about the waxing and the pre-workout. She did like to dive right into things as that was just her way, and usually it was fine and sometimes it was a disaster. The wax had been a small disaster and the pre-workout a slightly bigger disaster, but moving to Spain on a whim or getting involved with her ex's brother, that had the potential to become a massive disaster, didn't it?

"What do you really need right now, space to find yourself or to be shackled to another boyfriend?" Frankie asked her.

Lily blocked out all the protesting and encouragement

to do what was in her heart and tried to think. Hadn't she got blind drunk on the plane just at the sight of Mickey just a week and a bit ago? What was the time limit between relationships and rebounds? Was she just getting caught up in the excitement of it all, two men who seemed to be pursuing her? It was wonderful to have two gorgeous men texting her and wanting to see her. It was also wonderful for her ego to be on the receiving end of so much attention. It was just what she needed, in fact. But was she getting carried away with it all?

"You're fine, Lily. You do what makes you happy."

Was she though? Lily took a deep breath. "For months since the breakup I've been struggling to tell myself I'm fine. I've been so impatient to be fine. I really feel like I'm getting there."

"Of course you are!" Jan exclaimed.

Lily looked at Frankie, and despite all her friend's doom and gloom and weird ideas about relationships, she thought in this instance channelling a bit of Frankie's self-protectiveness might be good for her.

"But maybe I'm not there yet. I don't know."

The others looked at her in silence, perplexed. She knew it was hard for them to hear as they wanted her to be OK so much, and she loved them for that. And she was OK when you got right down to it. She was healing and changing, and the thought of running into Kiera McCrary and Mickey in the village didn't hold as much dread as it used to. She'd even managed to think about Kiera without adding in 'fucking' as her middle name.

"I don't know what I want," Lily said slowly. "Maybe it's Federico. Maybe it's Alex. Maybe it's not a boyfriend at all. But Frankie's right: I should think carefully before jumping into anything."

Frankie nodded. "Of course I'm right." Jenny threw a cushion at her face.

Denise looked uncomfortable. "Sorry, Lily. I guess we did get carried away with the whole thing."

"But it's only because we want you to be happy," added Lorna quickly.

Lily smiled at them. "I know. Don't worry, I understand." They knew how happy she'd been with Mickey during the good times and they wanted to see her like that again. But she could be happy without a boyfriend, too. After all, she was pretty happy right now.

Frankie nodded decisively. "Good. That's settled. Now, Lily, I've set you up a profile on this sugar website because if you're going to be single you may as well be earning."

They all stared at Frankie in horror. Lily felt her jaw drop open. Frankie stared back at them for several seconds and then said, "I'm kidding."

They all laughed in relief and threw even more cushions at Frankie, who hollered in protest that none of them knew how to take a joke.

When the squealing and throwing had died down, Jan asked, "One question, Lily: are you excited to see Alex when you get home?"

Lily pictured Alex's face. His warm smile. Remembered his hugs and the sound of his laugh. He really was gorgeous, and he didn't need Spanish sunshine or a foreign accent to make him enticing. She couldn't help but smile at the thought of seeing him again, and turned that excited smile on the others.

"You know what? I think I am."

CHAPTER SIXTEEN

On their flight out to Spain, arriving at the airport had been fun and exciting. As they all trudged into the airport for their flight home again Lily decided that there was no more dismal a place than an airport. There was no reason to stock up on magazines to read by the pool, no glasses of wine and toasts and enthusing about how good it was going to be to jump into the sea.

"This time tomorrow I'll be back at work," Lily said dismally and the others chorused that they would be working too, or at least returning to their responsibilities. Lily knew that she would be happy once she was back in her uniform at the restaurant, but just then she wished she could stay in Spain just a little bit longer.

Frankie brightened. "At least I have a trip to London with Mason to look forward to. He's flying me over the day after tomorrow."

Lily mentally planned her week. Work, a huge load of laundry and checking her bank balance, which was something she'd been putting off the whole time she'd been in Spain. There was her living situation to think about and whether she could afford her own place, or maybe sharing with someone. It would be good for her self-esteem to move out of her parents' place.

And there was seeing Alex. Her mind strayed over the memory of him just before Christmas. How he'd come to the restaurant's aid when she'd called him. Had that been because he liked her and wanted her to be happy, even when there was no hope for him as she was dating his brother? He'd always been so kind to her. Alex was a good person, a gentle person, and she wanted to make the right decision for his sake as well as hers.

The flight home wasn't as gloomy as it could have been as they all cracked open tiny bottles of white wine to have with their bags of peanuts, and Jenny found a ridiculous quiz in a magazine that had them all laughing. Lily was careful to stick to just two wines and walked off the plane with her own two feet.

They stepped off the plane in Belfast on an overcast afternoon and looked around at each other with tired smiles. There was no mistaking it. They were home.

"Look at the tan on her. Talk about a beach belle."

Siobhan's enthusiastic voice greeted Lily as soon as she entered the kitchen the next morning and she was hailed happily by everyone. Looking around at her fellow chefs and the familiar kitchen she realized she was glad to be back. It wasn't just the restaurant either. It was the village. It was her family. It was her friends. They all made up this place called home and she would have missed them dreadfully if she'd moved to Spain.

Lily pulled back her sleeves to show Siobhan the tan on her arms. "All natural, too. Didn't need to fake it after a few days."

The pastry chef made an envious face. "That's it, I'm booking. Any hot men where you went?"

"Who me? Notice the men? Don't be ridiculous." But she gave Siobhan a surreptitious wink so she'd know there really was gossip and she'd spill the goods when they had a private moment.

When the lunch rush was over she and Siobhan were cleaning up their prep areas and the others had moved to the far side of the kitchen. Lily leaned over and said quietly, "I got off with a hot Spaniard."

Siobhan shrieked with excitement until Lily motioned her to keep her voice down. "Who? How did you meet him? What was he like?"

As she filled Siobhan in on all the details, the other woman's eyes grew wider and wider. "You lucky, lucky bitch. I'm definitely booking a holiday somewhere hot and sunny now. That's exactly what I need, a hot little mover on the dancefloor and in the bedroom."

Lily laughed and felt her phone buzz. As she drew it out of her pocket she said, "You'll come back feeling like a new woman, I promise."

The name on her phone made her heart beat faster. Alex. *Can I take you for a drink or something after work?*

She typed back straight away. *Yes, I finish in half an hour if you're around then?* Damn it, Lorna would tell her she'd just done the wrong thing, that she should have made him wait and told him she was busy. But this was Alex. She didn't need silly games with someone like Alex. He wasn't a player.

His answer came through a moment later. *Perfect*

Siobhan was giving her a curious look but Lily put her phone away and kept on working. There was no need to broadcast it round the kitchen that she had a sort-of date with Mickey's big brother.

Half an hour later Siobhan let out a low whistle and called out, "That sexy electrician's hanging about outside, arse as cute as it always was. Mmm-hmm, I do like a tight pair of jeans."

Darryl looked up from his station in alarm. "Electrician? What's gone wrong?"

"Nothing! Bye!" Lily grabbed her bag and was out the door before more questions could be asked.

Alex was sorting through a toolbox in the back of his van when she approached, shaking out her hat hair. Maybe before she'd gone on holiday she would have stressed about seeing a potential date (crush? possible boyfriend?) straight from work but she had a newfound confidence and just didn't care. Alex wasn't the sort of man to expect a girl to be done up to the nines 24/7 either. Besides, he had cobwebs on the cuffs of his jeans. Neither of them were winning any fashion awards that afternoon.

He broke into a smile when he saw her and put the last of the tools away. "Welcome home. Did you have a good time?"

As they headed over to the pub she gave him an edited recap of their holiday, playing up all the sun and food and playing down the hot Spaniard and all the sugar daddy talk. Once they were ensconced in a corner of the bar with drinks, Alex became serious.

"I wanted you to know that I never knew about Mickey and Kiera. I've been wanting to tell you for months but it never seemed the right time to bring it up. If I'd known I would have fucking belted him."

It was hurting less and less every time she heard their names, something Lily was grateful for. She was also touched by Alex's concern. It really seemed to bother him that she thought he might have known what his brother was up to. "It's all right. I never thought you knew."

Alex seemed relieved. "When he told me about him and Kiera, all I could think was that I'd never, ever have done something like that to you. And that's when I knew I... I like you Lily. A lot. Always have, I guess. Since school."

He smiled tentatively and she felt a warm glow spread through her. He liked her. It was one thing to hear gossip and conjecture from her friends but it was quite another to be standing in front of a man while he confessed his feelings for her.

"Since school? I always thought you thought I was an annoying little brat." He'd been two years above her and Mickey

He grinned. "Well, you were. A funny little scrap of a thing with a cheeky smile. But then you grew up and I thought you were sweet and lovely, too. You went off to college and I thought you'd move away, and then you didn't. You came back. But in the meantime, you'd got serious with Mickey. He noticed you first. Always quick on the uptake, our Mickey. Quicker than me."

He smiled a sad smile at her and she could see how much he regretted that he hadn't spoken up when they were younger, and that his brother had hurt her like he had.

"So," he asked quietly. "What do you think?"

What did she think about dating him, being with him. She didn't know what she thought, but she wasn't letting him get away with that. "What do I think about what?" she asked innocently.

He grinned. "Going to make me spell it out? Fair enough. I'd like to take you out some time. I'd like … I'd like…" They were sitting very close together and he trailed off, looking at her. Then he cupped her cheek and lowered his mouth to hers. His mouth was very warm and gentle and she felt her toes curl. *Oh, that's a good kiss.* It was a very good kiss in fact, one she felt all the way through her body. She returned the kiss and then broke it, conscious of prying eyes in the bar. But she didn't move away.

Alex looked at her carefully. "Is it weird for you, me being Mickey's brother? Maybe I look too much like him, sound like him." He shrugged, uncertain.

Lily shook her head. It wasn't that exactly. Thankfully he didn't remind her of Mickey at all. And that was the important thing, wasn't it? No, wait, there was something even more important than that. Way more important than who he was and who his brother was. Lily remembered what Frankie had said to her while they were on holiday. She might be a moody, fussy complainer but Frankie did know a thing or two about self-care and boundaries, and Lily needed a lot of both right now.

So that was the million-dollar question: was she ready for another relationship?

CHAPTER SEVENTEEN

"Thank god the holiday's over and I can eat again," Denise exclaimed, looking between a plate of chocolate biscuits and a sponge cake and trying to decide which one to have. Lily thought of her double shift at the restaurant yesterday and how she'd been run off her feet and had barely had time to eat a carrot stick. It was four days since they'd all returned from Spain and tea and gossip was badly needed. Cake seemed like an excellent idea, too. The sponge was oozing with cream and strawberries and Lily helped herself to a piece. She'd earned it.

They were at Lily's parents' house and her mum brought them two big pots of tea and left them to it, but Nanna Maureen sat down with them and took a piece of cake too, saying, "I want to hear all about this holiday. Have some cake, dear," she added, offering the plate to Lorna.

Lorna shook her head, though she was looking longingly at the sponge. "Not me. Calories never take a holiday so neither do I."

Around a mouthful of buttery cake and cream, Lily said, "But it's sooooo good."

Seeing the ecstatic expression on her face the others dived in. Even Frankie took a small piece and ate tiny bites with a fork. By her elbow her phone was chiming away every other minute.

"Who's messaging you so much!" Jan exclaimed.

Frankie shrugged. "Some of the messages are from Mason, you know, the £800 Harley Street guy, and some of them are my new matches on these sugar dating apps."

Maureen perked up. "Sugar dating? What's sugar dating?"

Lily grinned and launched into an explanation. Nan was going to love this. "Frankie's only dating rich, older men now who shower her in money and presents."

Maureen nodded. "Very sensible, dear. Why give it away for free when you can be clever about it?" She peered over her shoulder and then winked at Lily. "Don't tell your mother I said that, she's such a terrible prude."

They all screeched with laughter and Frankie beamed at Maureen. "I'm glad someone understands."

"But how was the trip to London?" Denise wanted to know.

Frankie squared her shoulders and prepared to tell the tale. "Well, he flew me business class and had a driver pick me up at the airport—a Mercedes, and I was glad because men who favour Mercedes aren't tacky like men who prefer BMWs. I had a room booked in a hotel in Mayfair and he met me there when he'd finished work and we had cocktails and dinner.

It was very elegant and he's a gentleman. Paid for everything of course and sent me home with another £800."

They all stared at her, waiting for her to go on. Frankie looked around at them, confused. "What?"

"I'll ask seeing as no one else is going to," Maureen said. "Did you sleep with him?"

"On the first date? Certainly not. I'm a lady."

"You didn't even have to sleep with him!" Lorna exclaimed, "And you got *£1,600*?"

Frankie made a face. "Well, I still worked for that money. We talked for over seven hours and he was so, so boring. He only wanted to talk about his medical conferences and barely asked me any questions about myself. He spent an hour talking to me about a rival doctor who got some paper published before he did or something. I wanted to scream I was so bored. Then there's the travel time. 26 hours door to door is £61 an hour. He got a bargain."

£61 an hour. Lily put another forkful of cake in her mouth. When you put it like that it wasn't such a great deal of money after all, and if you have to put up with boring conversation… well, she'd take quiet drinks in the pub with people she *did* like, frankly.

"Oh, that does sound dull," Denise said, disappointed. "I wanted a glamorous tale that I could live vicariously through. Will you keep doing this or was that one taste enough for you?"

Frankie raised her eyebrows. "Are you kidding? I'm going

back in three days and Mason's going to take me shopping at Prada for a new handbag. I always knew men were dull, remember?"

Maureen hooted with laughter and clapped her hands. "To be young again! I would be doing the same thing."

It was a good thing her mum was out in the garden, Lily thought.

Jan turned to Jenny. "What about you, heard from Alonso?"

Jenny's eyes lit up. "Yes! We video-called last night. He's just the sweetest and he wants to see me again. The plan is for me to fly out and see him next month for a long weekend. High summer in Spain." Her eyes were dreamy.

Frankie gave her a shrewd look. "I hope he's paying all your expenses."

Maybe on holiday that would have upset Jenny, but she just gave her friend a smile. "He is."

"I'm so jealous," Denise said. "I won't get another holiday in ages. Can you put me in your hand luggage?"

They all discussed what they would be doing if they were in Spain at that very moment. Lily thought she'd rather like to be reading by the pool, or perhaps listening to Federico talk about this local cheese or that nearby vineyard. But she didn't really miss him. She'd got a little caught up with it at the time but he really was just a holiday romance. Something to pass the time in the sun.

Lost in her thoughts, it was a surprise to glance up and see that half the table was looking at her. She knew what they wanted to know: had she seen Alex? She gave a tentative smile and said, "I saw him."

Everyone stopped talking. Denise had been about to bite into a biscuit and she paused, biscuit hovering in front of her mouth. "And?" she asked, cautiously.

Lily remembered that kiss, how warm and delicious it had been. Comforting and exciting at the same time. The difference between him and Federico was clear now: Federico had been fun, but Alex was real. She was still trying to sort out her feelings for Alex and she wasn't sure she'd made the right decision. "I like him, I really do. So much. I always have. And I told him that when I saw him."

Jenny heard the "but" in her voice. "But not enough for a relationship."

Lily hesitated, and she remembered what she'd said to Alex yesterday, after he'd kissed her. *"I think if I do this I want to do it right. And right now, the time is not right, and you deserve better."* She was attracted to Alex. She liked him a lot, in fact. That one kiss was enough to show her that there was something between them, something real that could grow.

"Maybe there is. But not yet. It's too soon and I'm still figuring things out."

"Was he...upset?" Jan asked.

Lily had hoped he wouldn't be too disappointed, or hurt, or angry with her. And he wasn't. "He said he understood after everything that had happened why I needed some space right now."

211

"Ah, he's a good man," Denise said, biting into her biscuit. "I've always liked Alex."

Maureen nodded her approval. "I think you made the right decision, dear. Better to be cautious and take it slow if you're not sure that you're ready, than dive in and ruin something fragile. Maybe you'll be ready to try something with him in a few months or a year. Maybe you will have found someone new by then, maybe he will have. As long as you're making decisions based on what you want, not on what you think you need, then you're doing the right thing."

Lily smiled at her Nan. "Thank you. I think I made the right decision too. Alex and I are just friends, for now." Then she grinned. "But that doesn't mean I won't check out his arse occasionally in the pub."

"Atta girl," Lorna said with a wink.

"I wish we could go away again," Jan said wistfully. "My Instagram is dead right now with no holiday snaps to post."

This had been something else Lily had been thinking a lot about. How good it had been to relax and reset with the girls. She was a local girl through and through but that didn't mean she didn't want the occasional adventure to a far flung, exciting place. Lily sat forward excitedly. "There's no reason why we can't. Not right away of course, but we should start saving up and make this holiday a regular thing. We can go somewhere every year, just us girls."

"Yes!" Denise cried. "To save our sanity. This break from the family has been bliss."

The others chimed in excitedly saying how much they liked the idea as well, and started brainstorming ideas.

"Skiing in Switzerland. I always fancied myself as a bunny on the slopes," suggested Jan, the stylish photo opportunities in the snow and in front of open fires shining in her eyes.

"Island-hopping in Greece," countered Jenny. "We need sunshine and olives again."

Lily spread her hands on the table, looking around at them all with a wide grin. "I'm thinking we go even further afield next time. Bigger. More glamorous."

Frankie nodded approvingly. "I agree. Onwards and upwards at all times."

Europe was all well and good but there was so much of the world that Lily had never seen and she was hungry for it. If she'd learned so much by going just to Spain, imagine what she could discover by going even further afield. "I'm thinking Las Vegas."

They all squealed in excitement. "Vegas! Yes!"

"Think of the men in Vegas," Lorna said dreamily. "The fashion. The perving ops."

"The rich men," added Frankie.

Lily looked happily around the table. She'd had the trip of a lifetime with her best friends in Spain and learned so much about herself and what she wanted from life. It was exactly what she needed and she couldn't wait to do it all over again. Bigger, brighter, better.

Holding their cups up in the air they all cried out, "We're going to Vegas!"

ACKNOWLEDGEMENTS

My thanks go to the spirits in the sky: Jimmy Gray, Bertie Stevenson, Sammy Gray, Jeanne Kilpatrick, Rae Murdock and Roseleen D Mills (née Watson).

Also to all those local people from Cloughmills and surrounding areas who we lost in 2017 and 2018, and who have joined this mighty force in Heaven.

Special thanks go to my sister-in-law Jenny Gray, who put up with my changes throughout the writing of the book, and always took time out to read it and give advice.

And of course, thank you to my family: my partner Darrel Stevenson, who has never once doubted me or complained; my two sons, Tiernan and Robert (RJ); my little granddaughter Aria Rose; and of course my strong, beautiful mother Bernie Gray. I love you all.

I hope you all enjoyed the book, and I'll see you in the next one:

LOCAL LILY GOES TO VEGAS

Stephanie Gray

Stephanie Gray was born and raised in a small rural village in Northern Ireland, where she still lives today. She and her partner Darrel are both chefs, and they run the local village restaurant.

Printed in Great Britain
by Amazon